Tracks in the Sand

by

Doug Wakeling

Tracks in the Sand

For information address info@mickiedaltonbooks.com

First Printing 2014

ISBN: 978-0-9923422-6-5

Published by The Mickie Dalton Foundation
Kempsey, NSW
Australia

www.mickiedaltonfoundation.com

About the Author

Douglas Wakeling

Hailing from the mid north coast of NSW at Valla Beach, author Douglas Wakeling combines his passion for the written word, history and family ancestry. Since the late 1980s he has pondered over his family lineage, particularly the stories of John Joseph Layburn and James Fines his great grandfathers and their incredible journeys from England and Ireland to the country region of NSW, Australia.

While writing *'Curse the Bells,'* Doug lived in Maleny Queensland, noted for its excellence in the arts, which he puts down to the quality of the mountain air in the beautiful Blackall Ranges. He is a keen rail enthusiast and gardener and his venture into the literary world is sure to continue for years to come.

A Note From the Author

My Mother had moved from Dee Why in Sydney to the sleepy village of Nambucca Heads on the mid north coast to live in a retirement village in 1986 . I was having a quiet cup of coffee at home when the phone rang it was Macksville Hospital the message was that my mother had been hit in the main street at Nambucca Heads walking across the pedestrian crossing.

I jumped in the car and was there in twenty minutes.

"Mum what happened?" I said she was laying there in the casualty ward.

She replied, "I don't know. I was crossing the road when this thing hit me." She then hesitated and held my hand.

"Don't talk, save your strength," I said.

"No Doug, I have to tell you about my Grandfathers John Joseph Layburn .and James Fines," she whispered.

"Later, just get better," I replied.

As she lay there gasping for breath, she said, "Doug listen, there's an envelope in the bottom draw in the bedroom, it will tell you everything."

With that she closed her eyes and drifted off to sleep.

The Doctor on duty informed me she had broken both arms and six ribs and would have to go to Coffs Harbour into intensive care.

My mother went into a coma and never recovered. Six weeks later she was cremated in the Northern Suburbs Crematorium Sydney and placed in the wall next to our Father who had died in 1961.

The Layburn Chronicles

The Layburn Chronicles Part 1.

This story chronicles the life of John Joseph Layburn, from his humble beginnings in the small Hamlet of Otley where in his youth he was apprenticed to the famous Chippendale furniture makers, to his death in the new continent sixty years late.

A family tragedy causes him to leave his wife and children in England and set off on a remarkable journey. His adventures take him to the magnificent mighty Niagara Falls of British North America, the historical island of St Helena in the South Atlantic where Napoleon Bonaparte was interned and buried and finally to New South Wales.

On the way, our traveller is shipwrecked on Flinders Island near Tasmania.

John finally settles in the picturesque mid-west town of Carcoar which was to be his home for twenty years.

Although John does not allow the morality of the day to stop him from having what he wanted, he leaves a legacy of being a loving father whose indomitable spirit meant he was not afraid to take risks. When tragedy strikes, John demonstrates his courage in overcoming adversity and living life to the fullest.

The Layburn Chronicles Part 2

The story continues with John Layburn's son also called John, fighting at the battle of Elands River in the Boer War. John is with the NSW Citizen's Bushmen. In July 1900, they are sent to defend the supply depot at Elands River along with five hundred colonial troops. They were quickly surrounded by over six thousand Boers under the Commander, De la Rey.

Under heavy fire, they were sent a message by the Boer Leader to surrender. Lt Colonel Hore replied he would not surrender, that he is commanding Australian troops and they will cut his throat if he raises the coward's flag.

Finally, in August they are relieved by Lord Kitchener, who could not believe that the colonials had held their position for so long.

On returning from the war, it was reported in the Bathurst press that they had done their duty to Queen and country. Young John marries his sweetheart, Ellen Morris, the granddaughter of James Fines. His family lived in a wattle and daub hut near the Limekilns Hotel which nestles in the foothills of Mount Horrible near Bathurst. In the gold rush days it was a stage coach stopover.

James arrived in the convict ship. the *Medina* in 1823. After serving his time as a shepherd at Bathurst, he met his partner, Catherine Disney. Together they raised ten children, seven girls and three boys. His main claim to fame was a conviction for operating an illegal still in 1853. They were finally married three weeks before he died in 1863.

Dedication

My mother was tragically killed in the main street in Nambucca Heads, New South Wales in 1987.

This book is dedicated to Marcella Wakeling
MY MOTHER

Acknowledgements

Many thanks to:

Warwick Pullun for his thoughts on the early days of the Valla Gold Mine

Robyn Tankard for her permission to use her poem *"Mist in the Valley"* and

Leigh Stubbs for permission to use the cartoon *"Valla Flats"*

Table of Contents

	Page
William John Layburn	1
Valla Fishing Club	8
The Thongs I Have Seen	16
The Pink House, Oxford Falls	21
The Day That Changed My Life	27
The Passing Away of Jason Annear	33
Valla Gold	38
Madonna	75
God, I Hate the Cold!	77
Admiralty House	79
Popskie's Private Army	82
Mist in the Valley	85
Valla Flats	86
The Adventures of Chris	88

William John Layburn
Service No 5117
Rank Lance Corporal.

William John Alfred Layburn was born in Dunedin, New Zealand. He was the eldest son of John Layburn and grandson of John Joseph Layburn. He joined his father's wool and hides business and went to Australia in 1909 to obtain orders for his father and to gain experience as a wool classer. He traveled through New South Wales, Queensland, South Australia and Victoria. In 1915 he enlisted with the Australian Infantry Forces and was sent to France with the 22nd Battalion as a private. He was awarded the Military Medal in October 1917 for conspicuous courage and devotion to duty as a runner under heavy shellfire at the battle for Zonnedbeck in Belgium.

January 1917. Letter to his mother.

I don't think I will be long single, when I get back to Australia. No doubt the young lady I left behind is well on her way to being a Convert to our religion, so don't worry about me in this respect, Mother Dear.

After the war, I would like to know if you want me to come home first, before I go to Melbourne and perhaps get married very shortly after I get there. I am very much attached to this young Melbourne lady, for I consider her to be one in a thousand.

24th May 1917. Letter to his mother.

My fiancée has a school at Shepparton in Victoria and she writes to me once a week with nice cheerful letters.

Gee! She is a fine girl and I'm not sorry about my choice, for I am certain that I have done right and not made a mistake. That, I have absolutely made up my mind about.... Her name is Mabel Bliss...

Whilst he was staying in hospital and convalescing in England for a knee injury, William's fellow mates started to sing a popular song about *"My Mabel Waits for Me"* (song taken from a well known Australia poet). He was later transferred to the Australian General Headquarters.

William returned to the Front Line in mid-1918, where his Battalion was joined by the newly arrived 129th American Regiment. It was noted that the untested US troop's admiration for the Australian soldiers and deference to their judgment was almost embarrassing.

For two months William was involved in several fierce battles as the Australian forces pressed on to their target, the strategic town of Peronne on the Somme River. Getting close to their objective at the small village of Herleville, so depleted was the Battalion's fighting strength, that only with difficulty could a total of a hundred and twenty bayonets be raised. Of these, thirty had to be held back to be retained as reserves and the remaining ninety men were faced with the task of assaulting the German line on a front of over half a mile. Wave formation was obviously impractical and thin section groups were formed for the attack.

On the road which led into Herleville a few hundred yards to the right of the village and about four hundred yards in front of their posts, was a crucifix. The village and crucifix were connected by a sunken road, crossed in places by trenches and boarded on the far side by a high bank which served as a parapet for a strongly held trench. Around the crucifix there was a simple trench system.

William's Battalion orders were to occupy the sunken trench.

Taken from William's diary....

"Went over the top at 4.15 am. Big resistance from enemy machine guns....Ran the gauntlet of machine gun fire back to our lines and reported to Captain Pollington."

Taken from a letter to his mother dated 21 August. William explained what took place.

"Last Sunday morning, we went over the top and Fritz was waiting for us with dozens of machine guns. There were nine in our little party and we fought our way past a wood that was a nest of Hun machine guns. We got to a sunken road where we done a lot of damage. I killed four Huns myself and, as we were getting surrounded, we were forced to retire hurriedly and fight our way back. I was the only one of our platoon to come out alive and only four of our party got back. There were eleven of us left out of the company. The officers all reckon I was very lucky to

get out the way I did. I strongly recommended our Lewis gunner for a decoration and I hope he gets it.

The O.C. of our company has promised me promotion.

The 22nd Battalion History states, *"Of the ninety men who took part in the attack, sixty were killed, wounded or missing."*

But William's good fortune was about to run out. He wrote:

"On 25th August 1918, after a few days rest on the banks of the Somme River at Vequemont to re-equip and re-organize, the Battalion departed in motor buses. After a wet ride we de-bussed near some newly dug reserve trenches, about four miles from the firing line. The next evening we took over the freshly captured positions, just beyond the ruined village of Cappy. The Germans were fighting a rear-guard action, depending mainly on isolated machine-gun posts, established in some of the old trenches which were abounded in the area....there was little time for careful scouting...This constant advancing was terribly fatiguing as sleep was a luxury and the nerve strain constant... we engaged the enemy, wherever found, with bayonets, and we lost seven (killed in hand to hand fighting, in the dark)."

The Australian Commander, Lt. General Monash, determined to push the Germans backwards to the Somme River and capture some of the bridges. He ordered "aggressive patrols."

Setting off at six thirty am, William was part of a group sent forward to sort out the village of Dompierre, *"where a few Germans made a little show of resistance. They were soon mopped up,"* as he later wrote.

Monday 26th August. William wrote the final entry in his personal diary. *"Having good rest in trench. Hop over tomorrow morning. It is going to be a "big stunt."*

The ultimate object was the town of Peronne.

22nd Battalion History.

A further advance of 2,000 yards, was made on 28th August when Black Wood, on the outskirts of Herbecourt was reached. During the day an advance party of twelve was vigorously attacked by a number of Germans belonging to the Kaiserin Augusta Guards Regiment. They were splendidly led by a very brave officer who shot William through the head.

According to a report from the Battalion Adjutant, William Layburn *"was buried where he fell and a cross bearing his name and Battalion colors, now marks his grave."*

Records show his body was disinterred twice and then somehow lost.

The letter of condolence from his superior officer reads in part, *"He was taking part in the great advance and on the above date, when just outside Herbecourt, he was shot through the head by a German Officer."*

It was a severe shock to all his family back in New Zealand and his relatives in Yorkshire. William was a gentleman and he often spoke to his fellow mates of how he was going to return to Melbourne after the war and marry his sweetheart Miss Mabel Bliss.

One final thought

After the 1918 Armistice, a large number of remains were brought into Villers-Bretonneux town cemetery (known today as Adelaide) from small graveyards and isolated positions stretching out well beyond the town. They were without exception, those of the men who fell in the months from March to September, 1918.

Their remains were reinterred at 'Adelaide' in three large plots.

Plot 111 consists almost entirely of Australian graves, 250 being unidentified. William Layburn could be one of them!

On 2nd November, 1993, following a request by the Australian Government, an Unknown Soldier was exhumed from Plot 111 and reinterred in the tomb of the Unknown Soldier at the Australian War Memorial in Canberra. There is a possibility - admittedly extreme - that the remains of the Australian Unknown Soldier could be William Layburn of New Zealand.

Post Script. By Wilf Layburn, Wellington NZ. 2002

Some 75 years passed without any further clarification as to the final resting place of my uncle, William Layburn. I had a chance discussion with an official at the NZ Government's Department of Internal Affairs and he offered to initiate enquires through the Commonwealth War Graves Commission in Maidenhead, Berkshire. Within 48 hours, the name of William Layburn - but not his grave, was located on the Australian National Memorial at the Villers-Bretonneux Military Cemetery.

Villers-Bretonneux is a small town sixteen km east of Amiens, on the straight main road to St. Quentin. The actual memorial is on a ridge about two kilometres north of the town and honours Australians killed in France and Belgium, who have no known grave.

In January, 2002, as part of a personal pilgrimage to the Somme, retracing the well documented footsteps of William and my father, Ernest Thomas Layburn who also served in WWI, my wife and I visited the imposing Australian Memorial to the Missing at Villers-Bretonneux. A total of 10,982 names "Known unto God" are engraved on the screen panels, but just one name stood out on panel 96 that held my special attention, that of Layburn W. J. A. MM.

We also visited the hamlet of Herleville (today Hurleville) and were amazed to find the "sunken road" and bullet-scarred crucifix, a wayside cross, still exactly as described by William, 84 years earlier.

Having personally explored the Somme and gained a much better appreciation of the carnage and appalling loss of life during the Great War, I am now satisfied that William's burial site will never be located and that he lies forever in the soil of France

William Layburn, 1887-1918

On the 28th August 2014 William's story will be read out at the Australian War Memorial in Canberra.

Valla Fishing Club

The foundation members of the Valla Beach fishing Club were holding its first meeting at the headland of Deep Creek. The date was October, 1979. Those present were Jack Fisher (Mullet), Brian Stubbs (Flathead), Bobby Sullivan (Snapper) and Durango Smith (Black Fish). Brian's Ute was used as a platform for the table as notes were recorded.

"Look, thanks for turning up, fellers," said Mullet. "Gee, where do we start? My uncle is a member of the state fishing board and I ran it past him last night on the blower. I asked him for a wharf and boat ramp and could he organize to get the mouth of the creek dredged?

"His thoughts were, in his words, "Turn it up son, what you are asking for is a miracle, what do you think it is, bush week?"

Durango started to laugh and said, "Well if anyone can do it, Mullet you can."

The lads went on their merry way each weekend fishing in the creek and catching some amazing bream and flathead. It was in October 1980 that a special meeting was called at the same headland. All the members of the club were present and they had attracted some new faces. Jack Fisher opened the proceedings again.

"Members of the Valla Beach Deep Creek Fishing Club, I have some good news," he said. "I received a letter from the State Govt. and we have been given a grant of $200,000 to put into motion a plan for a wharf and boat shed."

There was complete silence.

"Well Mullet you take the cake," said Durango after a few moments. "We never thought you were really serious, and honestly I thought, ah well, let him go on another one of his hare-brained schemes."

Over the next twelve months the plans for wharf and boat ramp and jetty were approved and work started with a flourish. On the 21st of February 1981, the local Mayor, Gordon Pryor officially opened the wharf and boatshed with a great party.

The dredging of the mouth of the creek was a little bit harder. But the Fishing Club members applied themselves with great vigour. Sure enough, the river entrance was more difficult, but someone knew a plant operator in Nambucca. Gus was approached at the Rissole club (RSL) in Nambucca and was asked if he could do the job and how much. His answer was always the same, "Leave it with me she'll be right."

Gus made a start, said he would cut red and green tape corners and the creek was completed within six months.

They never did get the bill for the job. All they ever got from Gus was, "It's coming."

He is what you would call a bloody good bloke.

Over the next twenty-odd years, the Club went from strength to strength. They had over a hundred members and they even applied for a liquor license and were granted it, much to the distaste shown by the two licensed venues in the area.

The original four members, Mullet, Flat Head, Snapper and Black Fish were happy in the circus. Each weekend they would get in their twelve foot tinny and fish up the river past the rail bridge. It was always the same, a few cartons of home brew consumed on their fishing outings.

The Creek was silting up over the last few years and soon they would have to brave going out into the surf. Mullet would relate to the tale told by Pop Smith who used to fish the creek fifty years ago and he hooked a giant Jew Fish and when he finally landed it, it thrashed around in the boat. It was over five feet long and the boat nearly capsized.

Inset Left: The sign that caused the trouble

One weekend, a new member who had purchased a very fast jet boat decided to take it out into the surf. Everyone laughed and said he was mad. He was advised by the safety committee that the surf was too big and he should wait for the tide to change. But no, he was a smart ass and he was off.

He didn't last five minutes. The first wave hit and he flipped his $10,000 dream upside down. The members rushed out and saved the day and dragged the vessel back to the shore along with a very red-faced owner.

Mullet had been president for the first five years, it was his show, and he organized everything, Tag Fishing competitions, Wet t-shirt comps, everything. The list goes on and on.

Every Sunday morning the members would get together over a few cans and a BBQ lunch. The club had grown in numbers and it was not unusual to have a group of fifty members turn up. The fleet now had three deep sea cruisers that would regularly take tourists out for fishing trips.

It was an annual general meeting now, as the club had grown so big that they had to be incorporated and fear of litigation was always a threat. The date was October 1999.

The new president brought the meeting to order and when the formalities were completed the meeting was open to general business. Mullet got to his feet and proposed that the club put out a newspaper to celebrate the club's twentieth birthday.

A new member got to his feet and said, "What would you call this paper, would you seek advertisers, lastly what would you do with money raised from this hare-brained scheme?"

The President got to his feet and said, "I must admit Mullet, you do come up with some unusual ideas."

Mullet got to his feet and said, "The paper could be called *"Shark Attack - WOW!"*

"I like it, Neil Finney," Durango said.

Mullet continued. "Yes, thanks for that, Mate. It would get people in and yes, we would seek business in the towns around to advertise and money raised could go to the club plus a worthy local charity."

* * *

The Club had been up and running and was going flat out and they were getting to a stage where they had to close the membership as they had over a hundred members. The original four charter members had all taken leading positions and were now sitting back and letting the younger members take over.

At the annual meeting that year when the officer bearers had been elected, a new member from Urunga spoke.

"Thanks, Mr President. I have an idea that the club could buy a race horse. I have a mate who deals with young fillies and he says he can get us a good one for around $1000."

"That's great," said the President. "And how much would this nag cost to stable and feed, member Brian?"

"Well, it's about $100 a week for stable and feed," Brian replied.

The chatter from the members was going hell for leather. Finally the President rose and when the vote was taken, it failed.

Jack (Mullet) got to his feet and said, "Look fellers, we started this club to go fishing and we do that pretty well."

Then Bobby (Snapper) got to his feet, "Yeah, I'll second that, this club is starting to get off the rails! We're bloody fishermen not bloody jockeys."

There was loud cheering and the meeting came to a close.

The four lads were out on their weekly fishing trip one day. They had graduated from the creek to deep sea. Bobby Sullivan had purchased a Halverson Sea Gypsy, it was the latest in deep sea fishing, This Sunday, the ocean was like a mill pond, not even a gentle breeze.

Bobby broke the silence.

"Gee fellers, who do you think will win the Grand Final next week?"

Bobby always knew this would start a debate, as Mullet was a dyed-in-the-wool Manly Sea Eagle supporter and Durango was for the St George Dragons.

Brian broke up the subject before it could get started and passed around more Tooheys.

"Look friends," he said, "I'll come straight to the point. The club that we started back in '79 has got out of hand and I'm seriously thinking of pulling out."

The other three sat there in silence.

Then Durango said, "Gee I just got a big bite, I think it's a shark. Wow, there it goes again!"

"Well," Jack chimed in, "it's sad but I'm not happy either. It's getting out of hand, if you think back to when we started. I can't stand that milkman bloke, I wonder, did he have to train to be so obnoxious or does it come naturally?"

Then Brian joined in. "Look fellers, my job is going to take me away most weeks and the wife is starting to complain. She wants to go out on the weekends and she's sick of the same night out at the club every night. Anyway, we don't have any direct say now the new president has got his little click. God, the latest is no thongs or board shorts after seven pm! What will they come up with next?"

At a special meeting of the Valla Beach Fishing Club, the then President had called a meeting of the executive.

"Friends thanks for coming to this special meeting," said the President.

Those present were the President, Leonard Thompson, Secretary Simon Townsend, Treasurer Ben Ford and Bruce Gresham, the four members making up the executive of the Valla Deep Creek Fishing Club.

The members were grumbling as some of the long-time members of the club were now considering that the club was being run by a gang of four.

The President brought the meeting to order and called the Secretary to read out the business arising.

"Members," said Simon Townsend, "there is only one item to discuss at this meeting, that is, what disciplinary action do we take regarding Members Fish and Stubbs?"

Ben Ford, the treasure got to his feet and said, "They refuse to pay the fine imposed on them re the incident at the boat ramp last July. We can't have members flaunting rules. I say we cancel their membership."

The President got to his feet and put the motion to the meeting. It was passed by the executive members.

The news spread like wildfire and the members were soon raising a racket. But nailed to the notice board was the message that the two members in question had had their membership withdrawn and there would be no recourse.

The local press were at the club house wanting a response from the club management. Their answer was, *"No Comment."*

There was uproar by some of the members but in the end the club's executive won out and the matter just died away.[1] However, some time later, the members who had placed the sign (Picture, page 10) were dismissed.

---

[1] *There have been many incidences in the past where clubs like this have got off the ground through the efforts of a few hard working members, working weekends and nights with little help from the outside and no payments, then when it is up and running, others take over and run the ship.*

The Valla Beach and Deep Creek Fishing Club is fiction.

The Thongs I Have Seen

Most mornings I walk down to the beach and there they are, lined up all in a row. They are mainly rubber and all the colours of the rainbow.

I would walk down to the beach around 6.30 each morning, winter and summer. I have been lucky to see whales breaching in the surf in winter and see the sparkling waves in summer. I meet the same people each morning. There is the couple with three dogs and the lady with two dogs. They all go through the ritual of removing their footwear before going on their walk. They all head north towards Oyster Creek.

It's usually the same each morning, I say hello as they pass going up or on their way back, never too much to talk about except the weather or that the weekend looks good or do you think the wind will come up, or it might rain.

Then there is stick man. He must leave home before dawn. He never misses, no shoes and you can tell his path by the footprints and the mark made by his staff. He was always good for a talk on the latest political situation.

Some mornings, now and again in the summer around nine

am, I would venture down the bush track and walk north. All the early morning walkers have been and gone but lately there has been a pair of pink thongs all on their own. I am a bit nosy and curious and I could see this person walking down the beach about three hundred yards ahead of me, so I followed, not thinking anything in particular. Then all of a sudden the person was gone. I had deduced she was a female. She had long blond hair, although that does not tell you anything these days. It was not hard to see where she had left the beach as her footprints were visible in the hard sand, so I followed the trail up into the sand dunes, and there she was swimming in the back creek stark naked. God, she was lovely! I backed off, and walked back along the beach and sat on the seat.

It was early November when I followed her at some distance down the beach. It was a magnificent day, surf gently rolling into the shore, then something strange happened. The girl turned and waved. I continued to walk up and followed her in on the track that led into the back lagoon, there she was about to dive into the sparkling water. By the time I reached the water she was swimming gracefully out into the deep part. The water runs alongside the railway track and the XPT passed on its journey south.

I stripped my shorts off and dived into the clear water. It was fresh but it was like Blue Lagoon out of the movie as I surfaced next to her.

I said, "God, you're beautiful!"

We frolicked around for a while then we lay on the grass verge in the sun.

"I must go," she said. With that she quickly wrapped a sarong around her midriff. Her uptilted breasts, God they were perfect and they sparkled in the morning sun. As she

17

left the back beach, she called out, "I'm here most days!" She said she lived in 17 Smith Street Valla Beach.

My last view of her was her swaying hips as she crossed over the dune and she was gone.

Well, in for a penny, in for a pound. It was not far to 17 Smith St. and I arrived there just after dark, climbed the steps to the front door and knocked.

"Yes, who's there?" came this rough voice.

"It's me, we met down the beach this morning."

"Sorry sonny, wasn't me and I live alone here, you've got the wrong address."

Well, I left there with my head low and walked home. I mumbled to myself how I got that wrong.

Next morning I set out for the short walk to the beach. It was early but sure enough there they were again, pink thongs all alone not a living soul on the beach, was I dreaming or going mad? I quickly marched along the sand. It was a beautiful morning not a cloud in the sky, just the hint of a gentle breeze. It was easy to follow her tracks in the wet sand and as before they turned and went over the dune to that water hole. There she was lying on her towel, naked

The first thing she said was, "You didn't turn up."

She turned and her golden hair fell over her face. God, she was gorgeous.

"Babe, I went around and you weren't there."

With that she raised her body up and walked down to the water and dived in. Just as she hit the water a passenger train went by. I stripped down to my undies and dived in and came up beside her.

"Look, tomorrow morning as the sun comes up, meet me around the corner, just past the rocks, I'll be there and will show you my nest," she said.

"What about Smith Street? Are just kidding me to see if you were for real?"

With that, she climbed out of the water, placed the sarong around her body and left. She waved and she was gone. I quickly left the water, dressed and raced after her but as I climbed over the low dune and looked, she had disappeared. Strange.

The sun was just creeping over the horizon as I reached the bottom of the walk way the next morning and to my surprise, no thongs. So I looked up and down the beach but there she was on a rock just near the water so I walked towards her. She turned and in a flash she was gone .When I reached the spot there were footprints so I followed them. The tide was up so I had to wade through water up to my knees. It's as if she just disappeared but there she was standing at the entrance to her cave.

Well, I kid you not, all that summer I was down the beach each morning. I was like a kid in a lolly shop. Then all of a sudden, it stopped, the pink thongs were gone. I searched all that day and all that week but no golden goddess. I searched the cave but nothing. She just disappeared. Had I been dreaming?

As the years roll on, each morning as I walk along the beach, my eyes are looking for those pink thongs.

I'm now in my 70s but it keeps me going each morning looking for those pink thongs.

The Pink House, Oxford Falls, NSW

Roma and I were married in 1960 and after our honeymoon in Melbourne we moved into a garage flat in Kangaroo St, Collaroy Plateau on the Sydney northern beaches. When our first son was born in April 1962 we were on the lookout for a bigger accommodation. Our landlord Mr Ford had an egg run and he got them from an egg farmer in Oxford Falls, which is a rural community near French's Forest. So we moved into the Pink House, just over the falls in Oxford Falls Rd.

All of a sudden we had a house with room to move. Our new landlord, Noel Spicer would play a big part in our life over the next ten years. As our first son Peter grew and really enjoyed the country air he ventured out one day and put Roma in a panic. The police were called out and they finally found him with a lad the same age down at the falls. Then twelve months later, he wandered off again and this time Noel and the police found him asleep across the road in a hen house. It did not take long for our landlord Noel to visit us. He would call in on his way back from his weekly shopping in Manly and have a cup of tea with Roma.

It was one of those visits when Roma shouted out to Noel who was down pulling out weeds in the creek.

"Noel, have you seen Peter and his mate, they were here only a few minutes ago?"

"No Roma," he called out.

It was another half hour when Roma started to panic and decided to get help. They were a pair of buggers and only five years old.

Roma raced up to the next farm and rang the police. Sergeant O'Farrell and his constable were stationed at Forestville. Noel had quickly rounded up some help and he and Ken Rigby and with the police had soon put out a search along the creek.

Noel said to the police, "Let's hope the little buggers did not cross the road and go near the falls, it's a good hundred foot drop to the bottom."

Then out of the grass, all covered with farmer's friends and soaking wet, the two little fellers emerged along with Lady Peter's dog.

Young Peter called out, "Hullo Mr Spicer, gee we were brave, you should have seen the big black snake we seen but Lady chased it away."

Noel soon had the two lost souls back with their mothers.

Peter was growing up fast and he was born the month after his Grandfather died on the 17th April 1962 and he put the life back into his gran. It was also in the August of that year that his cousin was born, so she had two new babies to spoil. We would venture into Manly to see her as much as possible and as Peter grew he would love to watch out for the Mobile service station to see the flying red horse.

Peter was on the move again and this time he ventured on his own over Oxford Falls Road and into Mr Griffiths' poultry farm. The police were called out again and Noel again found him asleep in a chook shed. Roma was raging and Noel stepped in to save the day. We enrolled Peter into a kindergarten in French's Forrest. He enjoyed it the first day but the second day as I stopped to open the gate he was out of the car and raced home. Noel would take him to the tip on occasions and Peter would return home with a hat or a hand bag for his mother.

Our second son Steven was due on the 12th Jan 1965 according to the doctors. As I was working at the North Sydney Leagues club, it was New Years Eve and a mate who lived in Beacon Hill, Wally Cockhedge was there also. We both worked at the club, so I left Roma and Peter with his wife Carmel, they were going to have a quiet celebration.

Steven had other plans and late in the night, Carmel took Roma to Manly Hospital. The leagues club was doing a roaring trade and about 1am Wally and I proceeded to drive to a party. It was then that Wally informed me that Roma had gone to hospital, he thought at the time not to inform me as I could not do anything.

We left the party around 2am and proceeded to drive home. When we reached Wally's place, Carmel congratulated me and told me I had another son. Steven came into the world with a complaint called thrush, his testicles were the size of oranges. Peter was with his Gran in Manly and he discarded his dummy as he saw an Elephant on TV with one and somehow Gran talked him into giving his up.

One of our disappointments in Steven's first year in growing up was there were never any photos taken (sorry Steven).

Roma was working at the egg farm owned by Ernie Flew and arrived home one Sunday with about a hundred chickens. The egg farm would hatch out their chickens and the cockerels would be drowned and only the hens were saved. Roma being a great animal lover made poor Lue

Bailey put them into a box and Roma would arrive home with a new venture - we were going into the chicken business. Yes we did raise some, the foxes got a few and that venture didn't last.

A friend of my mother's, Mrs. Gordon who lived in Harbord had somehow captured two scrawny pig suckers, so Noel and I picked them up and we fattened them up. Noel was milking a cow so they were fed on milk each day and they quickly put on weight.

Noel arrived at our place one Saturday afternoon to tell us about a property that could be for sale, so we drove on up to see the property that had been abandoned. It was Lot 1062, Oxford Falls Rd. After much searching we tracked down the owner. He was a Dutchman called Jacobs Johannes Zwanaveld. We tracked him down through the Dutch Embassy in Sydney. We agreed on a price of $800 to transfer the lease and the yearly amount was $24.00. It would be appraised every seven years and yes, it was due. They raised the yearly rental to $84, which we still thought was a pittance.

So our time at the Pink House was coming to an end, great memories but it was time to move on.

The big day came around and Lue Bailey brought his truck around and we moved the 400 yards up the road. Roma was working at the egg farm that day and we were going to have roast duck for lunch. Lue had prepared the duck and Roma had it in an electric fry pan all morning while she was packing eggs. It did not take long for us to move our furniture up the road and up the steep track. Since our first visit to the block someone had stolen the water tank. We all sat down to get into the roast duck.

Poor Roma, you needed an axe to dissect the bird, even Lady the dog wouldn't eat it.

Roma and the boys went by train to visit Roma's father and Stepmother in Melbourne. This gave me a few weeks to somehow get the two rooms liveable.

We were happy on our plot. We had a cow called Bess that kept racing off down the road to Lue Bailey's Bull. It was an Ayrshire with a twisted horn. It came into calf and we had built a proper milking sty. Roma loved horses so we had stables and rented them out and life was good for a while.

Our previous landlord, Noel ran a very successful poultry farm. His hobby was the Trots. I went with him on the odd night, he was also into the Dogs at Wentworth Park and someone talked him into buying two dogs, their names were Blinky Moss and Noel Moss. Now I kid you not, if you owned a hundred dogs, to get a dog to run at the Sydney track was a feat. Noel not only achieved that but Noel Moss won five races on the trot.

Roma had a Dachshund bitch and we were travelling around showing it. I was working for Johnny Pryor at his nursery in Belrose, his neighbour Fred was a Dachshund dog breeder. One day Roma arrived home to find her dog had climbed out the laundry window with the lead around her neck and hanged herself.

There was five acres of typical goat country. We cleared most of the land and put in a crop of peas. But our friend Lue arrived one day with a small pig so we were into the piggery business. Life was good on the farm.

The Pink House, Oxford Falls. NSW

Oxford Falls today is full of church schools and the old one teacher primary school is now a peace park. There is a set of traffic lights. It's just not the same.

The Day That Changed My Life

Sunday 17th August 1997.

"WHAT A GREAT DAY FOR A PICNIC!"

What a great day, the sun was shining brightly and spring was just around the corner.

We were part of a regular walking group that would venture out each Sunday morning to somewhere around the mid north coast. Today we were going out to explore the walking trails at the Promised Land near Bellingen for a game of Cards and a BBQ. The Promise Land is where the rich and famous live. We were serious about our cards, we played Canasta 500, Oh Bother, you name it, we played it.

However, first we had a quick car job at Azalea Ave in Coffs Harbour. Carol had picked up the necessary items; oil, new filter, etc., because we were going to do a quick oil change on her car. (Looking back Carol, we should have shouted you an oil change at a service station).

I had arrived at Val's place at 9am in Azalea Ave. Lesley said it was easy. ("Just undo the sump plug.") Mind you, Lesley was back at Elizabeth's place and had never changed the oil in her life. I was to pick them up after the car service.

We had borrowed a friend's car ramps. We had planned to do the job at Valla the following weekend. Anyway, I placed the ramps in front of the wheels and sat on the side wooden fence, Carol declined to drive the car at three minutes past nine, so Colin volunteered and he jumped in and drove the car up onto the ramp. He drove it up the ramp all right and went on over it and through the fence.

I called out, "Col, you're going too fast!"

27

The next thing I remember, I was lying on the bonnet of the car on the driver's side and somehow Col had veered to the left and then I was on the ground, my right knee hurt like hell and the car careered on onto the neighbour's front steps. I was still on the ground, knee still hurting like hell. The car was a mess and so were the front steps, the fence would need some serious work, also.

In the next few minutes there was a sea of people around, Ambulance, Police and tow truck. The next thing I knew, I was being placed in the ambulance and driven to Coffs Harbour Hospital, the pain in the leg still there. Straight into the casualty ward, X-rays taken, all I could think of was that they had to cut the leg of my new jeans off and was Colin all right?

While recovering in the Out Patients, my leg was being examined by a young Chinese intern as I thought, except it was Dr Chan one of Australia's leading orthopaedic surgeons. The x-rays confirmed that I had broken the Tibula Plateau and there was ligament damage and a small graze next to the knee. My leg was placed in a brace, as the surgeon couldn't operate till the abrasion healed and I was moved to "A" ward.

The characters you meet in hospital! Lennie lent me the Sunday papers and his portable radio to listen to the football. While this was going on I could not pass water, in goes a catheter (number 1). Lennie would tell the other patients in the ward about his budgie. He also went on about a certain Doctor in Macksville and how he was a radio operator in the war, and then he would go on and tell them how he helped this young fellow with his radio (me). He would ramble on late into the night.

My Nurse Nightingale came regular and my first visitor was Bill Nelson. I asked him if he would mind closing the window and he jammed his thumb. Sorry Bill!

Dr Chan had advised me that the leg should be set in plaster as soon as possible because of the ligament damage and a new knee joint would be fitted some time down the track (it was fitted 24th April 2008). First thing Monday, up to Coffs Harbour radiology in the ambulance for an ultrasound then back to "A" ward, leg now set in plaster

Next visitor was Peter Shales with a get well balloon from the Valla Lions Club. Meanwhile, two emergency patients arrived and the hospital needed my bed, then my Solicitor arrived to take particulars down for an insurance claim. I was moved to the TV room in a wheelchair the first catheter removed and I was again trying to pass water. My solicitor was trying to take notes.

They have found me a new bed in "K" ward.

The time is now 2.30 pm and Elizabeth and Lesley have arrived to pick me up. I was now going home.

Can't go yet, can't pee, and have not passed my licence on the crutches yet. (No one fails).

3pm, more visitors, I was still trying to pee into the bottle under a blanket.

Val, Carol, John Howley arrived. Still couldn't pee. Physio arrived with crutches, Junior Doctor arrived to tell me if I haven't peed in fifteen minutes, in goes a new catheter.

With all this activity and trying to pee under the sheets in a bottle, four visitors, what can a man do?

I told the young doctor there was a relaxing drug to make the bladder work. Here I am telling the doctor about the use of Valium, and I can't pee lying down with four visitors watching. Finally they left. Bingo!! Two litres! It was now 7pm but too late to go home.

Wednesday 12 noon, picked up by my Nurse Elizabeth and back to Ibis Drive. (Elizabeth told me later that the Doctor said that fifty years ago, the leg would have come off)

Thursday appointment with Dr. Chan at his surgery. He now thought he should operate as soon as possible. He produced an electric saw to cut a window in the cast, so we can continue to treat the graze. He had me worried, but he assured me he would stop when he saw blood. Actually the saw vibrated not rotated, so the skin was never touched.

He had programmed the operation for the following Monday.

All that weekend I was trying to get used to the cast, if that is possible. Monday afternoon, back to Coffs Hospital. As the admission centre is now at the bottom of the Hospital I could not negotiate the steep incline, so the Admission Sister asked Elizabeth to take her father to the Casualty entrance at the upper level. (Father!!) I called out to the young nurse. If I wasn't stressed before it was that event that made my day.

Finally allocated a bed in "B" ward, beds B1, and B2, Bananas in Pyjamas, the young fellow in B2, had been involved in a bike accident. I was now scheduled to be operated on Tuesday. Monday was a bad day.

The patient in B2 was in bad shape. His wrist was so bad that the doctor had taken delivery of a special brace. The Doctor had taken it home to look it over and read the instructions. B2 assured me it would be his last bike race (I wonder).

Tuesday, the operating theatre was full and the graze had not healed enough.

Let me tell you about "B" ward. We were opposite the sterilizing room and the bed pans sounded like a Chinese Laundry. I couldn't sleep so they shifted me to "K" ward.

My fellow roommate in "K" ward had a special problem that couldn't be put into words. He had a permanent erection, it would not go down. I tell you, he was not laughing.

Wednesday, the operation was put off till Thursday.

Thursday Big Day, what else can go wrong?

My surgeon visited me in the afternoon on crutches, something about throwing something at a cat, he assured me he could operate sitting down. At 5pm, the anaesthetist arrived. He asked me if I had I any questions. I said, "Yes please wake me up after the op."

Anyway, the leg was prepared for operation at 8pm and I was wheeled down to the theatre. They couldn't find the X-rays and the cantaler (WHAT'S THIS?) had to be replaced as the old one wouldn't work.

Sometime in the early hours I was wheeled back into the ward with my thumb on the button. Each press administered a small dose of morphine. There was a safety system so you couldn't overdose.

I now had a new cast, a plate and two three-inch screws inserted, and it hurt like hell. It was tight and there was a new problem - I have not peed since before the operation. You guessed it, another catheter and they have kindly cut a new window in the cast where it was killing me. By this time, I had lost count of the catheters.

The weekend was a bit of a blur. Many visitors, still no visit from my ex wife but my Nurse Nightingale regularly visited twice a day. I can't remember when the catheter was removed. It was now the first of September and the talk was that Princess Di had been killed in a car accident. Elizabeth fobbed it off, she said she had not heard. Didn't want to upset me. Elizabeth brought me a book called *"The Horse Whisperer."* I could not get past the first chapter. The story is about a girl riding a horse and is run over by a truck and has her leg amputated.

Tuesday morning, a visit from Physio. Tried to walk on crutches.

Wednesday, more lessons, I walked up and down the stairs. One look at the fire escape stairs and I promised myself I would not visit anyone with stairs. Anyway, four steps up and four steps down. I passed. No one fails.

Wednesday afternoon, I was picked up by Elizabeth and taken back to Ibis Drive, Toormina.

It was six weeks before the cast came off and my leg was fitted into a brace and I was still on crutches.

There were many genuine friends who came to visit me over this period including Carol and Val with a six pack. God, grog was the last thing on my mind!

I never would have made it without my Nurse Elizabeth; we were married at the town of Carcoar NSW in August 1998 where my mother was born.

We never got to go to the Promised Land for that picnic. Perhaps one day!

The Passing Away of Jason Annear

As a long time supporter of Manly Rugby League, I attended my first game at Brookvale in 1947 and spent my youth surfing at Queenscliff. I was saddened to read about the death of a young promising footballer.

The body of 21 year old Jason Annear was found at the base of Queenscliff. It is believed he fell to his death while returning to his home in Collaroy after the Manly Warringah presentation night. He was a rising star and was on standby to make his debut to play with the Manly first grade team.

Club officials said it does not make sense. He was a quiet kid extremely polite and absolutely no trouble.

He will be missed by our Club and our thoughts go out to his family.

In 1916 my Uncle Leonard Wakeling fell to his death at Queenscliff, aged sixteen. It was because of this accident the Manly ambulance was formed. The ambulance duty was a volunteer basis. A greengrocer in Manly whose duty was to retrieve patients was called to the beach and Leonard was taken to the Manly cottage Hospital.

It was well reported in all the major newspapers in NSW. The Sydney Morning Herald, Thursday 20 July 1916 stated:

"The death of Leonard William Wakeling, a clerk, which occurred at Manly Cottage Hospital on July 13, was the subject of an inquiry conducted by the City Coroner."

It was also reported in Adelaide, SA, Tuesday 18th.

Fatal Fall

Leonard Wakeling living at North Steyne, Manly, died in the Manly Cottage Hospital as a result of injuries sustained on Wednesday.

Leonard who with his mother and two younger brothers lived at 88 Ocean Beach Rd. Manly.

A Boy's Fatal Fall.

Leonard William Wakeling aged 16 years, living at Manly, was walking along the cliffs at Queenscliff Point, near Manly, on Wednesday 12th July. He was fishing from the rocks at Queenscliff. After tiring of a dull sport, he started to climb the cliff. When he reached a height of fifty feet, he slipped and fell backwards over the cliff. He landed on a ledge of rock about twenty-five feet below and then he rolled off and plunged another twenty five feet to the rocks. Apparently he lay there for about three hours because the amateur ambulance at Manly could not be summoned. But Dr. McVittie was summoned, did what he could for the lad as he lay there, and stood by him until he was finally carried to the Manly Cottage hospital.

The Manly police were informed by a companion, Sewyn Newth, and, after some trouble, with help from some lads, succeeded in conveying him to the Manly Cottage hospital, where he was admitted with a fractured right leg and possible internal injuries. There was no resident medical officer at this hospital, and the matron had only occupied the position for two weeks.

Leonard William Wakeling

When young Wakeling was admitted, she rang Dr Barron, gave him some details of the case, stated in her opinion that, it was not serious, and told the parents that it was not necessary to call in the Doctor.

That night he was in severe pain and in shock with a broken leg and internal injuries. All that night the parents stayed with the lad. At 9am the next day, Leonard was finally seen by Dr Barron who now finally realised the case was more serious than he had been told. Leonard died at 4 pm that afternoon. Doctors reported that he died from a broken spleen.

The story was briefly told in the evening papers. The inquiry revealed some other queer things. There were seven Doctors in Manly at this time, four of them attended patients at the Cottage but three of them were not permitted to attend patients there. The hospital was supported by public benevolence and State support.

It seems an extraordinary thing that, since Dr McVittie had attended the lad on the rocks, he was not able to give him attention at the hospital. It seem extraordinary that the matron who must hold certificates, could regard a case of this kind as 'not serious.' It seems worse than extraordinary that a dying boy could lie fourteen hours in hospital without medical aid.

At an inquest held at Manly on the 16th July concerning the death of Leonard Wakeling aged sixteen, it was stated that the boy was at the hospital for twelve hours before he saw a doctor. There was no resident Doctor at the institution. The lad's father made repeated requests that his son should have medical attention. The matron in charge had rang up one of the Doctors and was told that the case was not serious enough, but the Doctor told the matron what to do .There were only four doctors who were on the board who were allowed to see patients at the cottage hospital.

Dr Barron said that death was due to apparently to a broken spleen. He did not think it was possible to save the lads life.

The coroner returned a verdict of accidental death, but he said it was strange that the lad was left for over twelve hours without a medical man seeing him. He understood that it would not have been possible to save his life, but some relief might have been given him and his parents. He went on to say that the hospital should be enlarged, and a resident Doctor installed.

It was reported in *"The Sunday Times:"*
The inquest on the death of Leonard William Wakeling held at the Coroners Court, on Wednesday, disclosed certain facts that ought to make Manly sit up and take notice.

A scandal of this sort cannot be ignored. The public waits now to hear what action the hospital authorities are taking. The public must be convinced that in future every case admitted to the hospital will have prompt medical attention.

Valla Gold
Gold, Gold, Gold

Dick Marshall - who worked for William Buckman - was about three miles north of Deep creek searching for stray cattle that had bolted. He was in an area that was thick bush when he stopped to slake his thirst from his water bag. He was perspiring so he sat down on a rock and kicked some dirt, swearing away. He'd had an argument with his girl friend the previous night. Although he had little education, Dick was fascinated by the sparkle in the soil. He picked the rock up, gave it a closer look and placed it in his saddle bag. He was going to take it back and show it to his boss.

He reached the stables just after three o'clock with the stray bullocks.

"Hey, Boss," he said. "Look what I found up on that ridge near Oyster."

William strolled over. It was late as he wanted to drive his sulky over to his neighbour Marmaduke England because they had a good supply of moon shine. The Englands had a fine grape orchard coming along and he was hoping soon to open a wine shanty.

"What you think Boss, might be that gold you tell me about?" asked Dick but got no answer.

Next morning, William and Dick set out for Oyster Creek for a closer inspection. Dick could not stop talking about how they were going to be rich. The hill to the west was called Bellinger Peak (later called Picket Hill) and it was shrouded in mist. Dick would tell stories that the local Aborigines had told him how in the dream time, the bad men would hide out up there. It was called Bolla Nulla.

Although William had cattle up there, Dick was not going up there, he had heard too many bad stories. They progressed up the track that was now being used as a main road to the Bellingen River and beyond. It did not take long for them to reach the spot. At first, William was not impressed but as he dismounted from his horse, his head was spinning from the wine he had the night before and he tripped and fell.

Dick helped him up and said, "You better give up that debel water Boss, no good."

"You might be right, Dick," William replied.

Dick was a Maori had came over from New Zealand, he had saved William from drowning one day when Dick dived into the water and hit his head on a rock. He was out cold but Dick swam out and saved him. They were friends for life

"Eh boss, I'll boil the billy, got some good damper Bess made last night," said Dick.

William was thinking as they rode back to the homestead. He had collected a sugarbag full of sample shale and quartz. He knew a mate in Sydney he would send it down on the next steamer and see what would happen.

Dick said, "What you think boss, we might be rich?"

"Ah Dicky, me lad, you never know," William replied.

William had been granted thirty acres on his Crown Lands grant as the NSW Government extended the 'Limits of Location' north of Port Macquarie. The conditions were that they had to clear the land and be involved in farming activities. William in his first years grew sugar cane and tobacco. William also had a thriving herd of dairy cattle and pigs. They soon found out that sugar need a warm, frost-free climate.

A few weeks went by then William received a letter from Sydney. He had forgotten all about the sugar bag he'd sent to Sydney for testing

William was having his morning cuppa on the veranda when the local postman rode into the property with his mail. There were the regular catalogues for his wife and this letter. The postal service was delivered by a rider from Kempsey. As he passed Valla Beach he would place all the mail in a bag nailed to a tree. One of the locals would row down to the mouth of Deep Creek and hand deliver to the residents. One of the letters William received stood out it looked important. It was from a Mr Warden Duckat from the The Mining Registrar. The report stated that the sample test result giving two and half to three ounces of gold rate per ton. They were strongly advised to peg out the claim and have it registered.

William had been reading all he could find about gold mining in the country and soon realised that the gold would have to be dug out of the site, not out of a river or water course. So Dick and William, after pegging out their claim started the slow process of digging up the hard ground. After toiling all morning they were having a tea and damper break and Dick said, "Well Boss what do we do now?"

They both looked at the heap of soil and rock.

"Well Dick me lad, we now have to sluice it through a solution of water in a pan and the gold will settle in the bottom of the pan"

"Ah!" cried out Dick. "Water!"

So the boys packed up and rode home to return the next with a drum of water. When they arrived at the pegged out area, they realised they had to construct a shed and rig a water tank for sluicing the soil and shale. It was hard work and after a few weeks they had dug a hole ten feet deep.

They had arrived at day break. They were going to do some work till lunch time and then they had to get back to the farm. They had been neglecting the property.

"Look Boss, a Bandy-Bandy snake!" called out Dick.

This snake has peculiar habit of living underground and was aggressive when disturbed. Dick took one look at the lovely white and black bands. He was not all that keen on snakes and swiped its head off with one fell swoop.

The word soon got out that gold had been discovered in the Valla area. In 1888, a report n the local and city papers stated,

> *"A discovery has been made near Deep Creek in the county of Raleigh and parishes of Newry and Valley Valley, of a belt of country which contained mispickel quartz which had the appearance of being highly auriferous and supposed to be silver and gold bearing. A further application was made by Buckman and Marshall, the prospectors, for a mineral lease of 17 acres. Immediately five other gold leases were applied for. Buckman and Marshall sunk a new shaft west of there first, and at 40 feet struck pay dirt. There are thirty four mineral leases applied for around the immediate neighbourhood of the prospectors, including Verge and TB Larke. Some assays*

have been made of the stone, and gold found to be the principal mineral. The reefs are proved to be very hard work and the stone difficult to treat, so that it can only be by great expenditure of capital that the field can be made payable. There is no machinery or other appliance on the field up to this for crushing or developing the mines. The gold in the stone is very fine dust."

In 1889 the Nambucca Gold and Pyrites Company was formed to work the mine for gold. (Eventually this Company was the only one to gain any successful results, the adjoining leases had negative results.)

That year the Company had put down a shaft to 105 feet, with drives bearing east and also west. Only on the prospector's lease Number 196, had gold bearing stone been struck. Assays from this stone were obtained, ranging at the rate of from five to seventeen ounces per ton with one reported to have been 33 ounces. About ten tons of stone were sent to Swansea (near Newcastle) for treatment, and twenty tons more stone were lying bagged up at the wharf ready for shipment if the return from the first proved satisfactory. Steady work was being carried on and a considerable financial outlay had been made on the lease.

Lessee Number 227 south of the prospectors had gone down 61 feet without reaching stone, but the water had come in so strong upon them that they required machinery erected to enable them to keep it under control. At that stage, there was no machinery whatever on the leases. All the raising and bailing was done with windlass and bucket.

By September 1891 the Gold rush was on big time. Eager prospectors were flooding in to join the bonanza, but it was not like Bendigo or Ballarat.

It was hard work and some of the names joined in the search there were Dalahanty and Co., Princess Dagmar Gold Mine, Cochrane and Neil, Southern Cross, Skoboloff and Partners, G.M. B.Lark and Nambucca Heads Gold Mine Co. Anderson and Co. was crying foul as someone had interfered and shifted their survey pegs.

There was a tent city with a General Store Bakery along with a hotel called the 'Morris Hotel' run by George Morris and a post office. It wasn't long before the wrong element arrived at the gold field. By 1892 there was a depression and nobody had any money. Married men came to work the mines leaving their love ones at home, It was soon apparent the gold had to be processed on the site so all the various companies built a chlorination shed and a dam was soon dug.

The following year Buckman subdivided his claim into 250 shares which were reported to have sold for £70 each. Surface ore on this claim yielded five ounces of gold to the ton after treatment, and at the 70 ft. level, the yield was thirteen ounces to the ton, by assay and three ounces of silver.

The Nambucca Heads Gold and Mining Company had their main shaft sunk to 200 feet with drives west, south and east at the 190 feet level. The value of gold at that time was thirty five pounds seven and threepence per ounce. They were in the course of constructing a plant at a cost of £5000, consisting of chlorination works with all the necessary machinery on the ground for treatment of their own ore, a full plant with rollers, stone crushers with screens and elevators etc. Plant was ordered for hauling and pumping, Electric lights were installed and forty men employed.

The Derrick at Valla

1892 was the best year for gold returns.

Although the Nambucca Heads Gold and Silver Mining Co. put through their chlorination plant 1235 tons, yielding one oz of gold to the ton valued at £4,986, the Company proposed taking the load to a greater depth.

Of course, the news of gold brought a few bad characters into the district.

Marmaduke England and a few locals fell for the three card trick, when they brought shares in a reef that had been 'salted.' The gold in the reef had been fired into the quartz by a shot gun and the reef was a dud and worthless.

The hotel at the mine was doing a roaring trade this Thursday night when one of the local farmers overheard a chap at the bar talking about their luck in Kalgoorlie in far off Western Australia, how they found gold just lying on the ground waiting to be picked up. He introduced himself as Bill Johnston and he got the attention of the local lads from Valla. A young stockman who had just been paid after doing a ten day's job droving a mob of cattle from over the range to his father's property near Macksville, he was all ears.

A deal was done, the lads from the gold fields in Western Australia had talked two young fellers into looking into a claim. So bright and early next morning, the four men set out up the main track. It was well marked. The leader was Bill Johnston and his side kick Dennis Brand who didn't say much. They had left as the sun was coming over the horizon and they followed the track that was becoming a major road linking the North and South. The temperature was warming up and the birds were in full flight, the parrots were going at full throttle screeching their heads off.

"We turn here boys, up this ridge," said Johnston.

They travelled for about three miles across gullies and tropical palm valleys.

"How much further Boss" cried out James.

"Not far now boys, another hundred yards then we turn right," replied Johnston.

When they reached the designated spot they dismounted and tied the horses to whatever was around.

James said, "I'll boil a billy, that was hard and thirsty work."

They were puffed out so they sat on a log and James said "Where's the gold? I thought it would be just lying around like you said it was like in WA."

Bill's offsider who had been quiet up till now said, "Look it's not that sort of gold country, it's in the rocks."

So after they had drunk their tea, Bill walked and the others followed down the short path down to a rock wall. Bill and Dennis had come up days before and fired gold dust into a rock crevice. James was at first sceptical as he had been warned that gold shysters could quiet easily pull a fast one. Danny who seemed to be the brains behind the scene pulled out of his saddle bag some papers. He had it all.

"Look fellers," he said. "We can do this the easy way or you can take it to your legal friends and that could take days. We're pulling out this afternoon we have to meet some other prospectors in a place called Urunga. They showed some interest when we called on them last week."

Although James was at first wary of the whole thing, he looked over the documents and the bill of sale and said to his friend John, "What do you think John?"

Johnny looked at the papers and turned them over and said "Well why not? There's gold around here, it might as well be here as well."

Then James turned the tables on the boys from Western Australia and said, "Look, let's not be too hasty about this. You go off and see the lads in Urunga and we will be waiting for you back at the Morris Hotel and we will have an answer for you. I want to talk it over with my Uncle."

With that, Bill and Dennis rode off in a huff leaving the lads behind.

James called out, "Don't forget, we'll see you back at the hotel."

John said to him, "Well what you think, we could be rich?"

James stopped and turned his horse. "John the only ones that were going to get rich were our friends from WA. That site was salted. I was lucky to have a talk with my uncle Marmaduke England. He lost money on a claim just like that." [2]

Despite considerable work going on, the year of 1893 saw The Southern Cross Mining Co. go into liquidation. They had sunk a shaft 150 foot deep but their lease was quickly taken up with a syndicate eager to try their luck

They had expensive pumping gear at work, but were unable to cope with the flow of water. A new shaft was sunk farther east. Over £ 2,000 was expended on this mine, but no auriferous stone had been struck yet.

David Anderson and party were working about 200 yards west of prospectors. They were also having difficulty coping with the influx of water, as was the Mr Friedlander and Party lease. Production ceased in 1893

In the following years there was little interest in gold mining except for a few men prospecting at Deep Creek. The plant and chlorination works were valued at around £14,000.

In 1894, Mr Marmaduke England wrote to the local paper that the mining adventure had collapsed because of poor prices for gold and the influx of water in the shafts.

---

[2] *Some years later a syndicate led by Powell mined that same rock face and took a quantity of antimony and small amount of gold and silver.*

There were only the road side inn and three families left in the area and finally the Post Office were closing.

Arsenic in big quantities was being recorded with its general use mainly in the control in the Prickly Pear outbreak. Nambucca Exploration Company was employing eight men raising arsenic ore for treatment by the Leggoe process.

In 1919 there was a resurgence of mining at Valla. A new player, Valla Gold Mining Syndicate commenced operation. The new syndicate set out to reopen the old workings. The old shafts had collapsed, so new shafts were put down to a depth of 140 feet and drives put out in a south easterly direction with an average width of fourteen feet with an average of one and half ounces of gold and 33 and half ounces of arsenic per ton.

In 1921, Valla Gold Mines were registered in Victoria with Victor Leggoe taking over the major interest. With this new capital they extracted 329 tons of Arsenic pyrites and 138 tons of arsenic was obtained

Work over the next five years was carried out the erection of a treatment plant and the manufacturing of bricks for furnaces. Nevertheless, a considerable amount of gold and arsenic was obtained.

In November 1925 there were six men working on the surface and seven men underground.

The Valla mining operation seemed to be always on the back foot and on the 30th May 1926, mining ceased as a result of the cost of transport, increased cost of production and the low price for arsenic.

In January 1928, the new owners of the mine were P. and C. Chemicals Ltd. They raised £75,000 in 150,000 shares at ten shillings each. So the mine was reopened in

1929. It was stated in a report to the stock exchange that Australia used over 3,000 tons of white arsenic per year. Orders of 700 tons were placed with the Valla Company. They were now looking for sixty men to be employed as miners at sixteen shillings a shift. They also needed shovelers, furnace men, labours, plant attendants and packers. Wages were low and risks taken by miners were high. A fifteen year old boy was employed to lead a horse forward and backwards for 55 hours a week in rain or sunshine received two shillings and sixpence per week.

But again in 1932 the company was forced into liquidation

In 1934 and 1935 the mine remained idle but in 1936 a new company Pacific Development Ltd. was formed to reopen the mine

In WWI, James Freeman was all packed and ready to embark on his journey to Sydney to join up for his part in the war. The train line had just passed the town of Wauchope, the town band was there to see the local boys off to Holsworthy army camp in Sydney. The local school children were there to sing God save the King and the local Mayor was there to give them a send-off and give his good wishes. One of the school children announced that they would be knitting socks to send them to keep them warm, even the boys said they would help.

James embarked from Sydney on the 16th of March, 1916 on the *"Malakuta."*

James Stanley Freeman had served in the 2nd Light Horse and saw action in France. He had joined up October 1915. He finally ended up with the 5th Pioneer Division

Ammunition Column, this unit was formed in Egypt. They were mainly Tradesmen Miners and Craftsmen and they were responsible for building bridges and plank walkways. He received three war medals, the 1914/15 Star medal, the British war medal 2/37 and the Victoria medal 36320.

He was discharged on 9ᵗʰ Sept. 1919.

The Australian Government were keen to see members of the AIF marry local English girls and they even sponsored their travel to Australia after the end of the war. There were numerous cases of bigamy. But James, age 24 married Nena Louse Emmett age 31 (Widow), occupation office worker. They were married at the Christ Church by the Reverend C.R. Bailey, licence no 288. Nena was to follow James out to NSW. James returned to Australia and went back to work at the family farm in NSW Pembroke near Wauchope.

On returning to Australia he had many farm jobs especially any work with horses. He was now a married man. He was home at his father's farm and was reading the local Port Macquarie newspaper and was taken in by an advert for mine works at a Gold and Arsenic Mine at Valla, about a hundred miles north. James wrote off to the Company and received a reply by the next post. He was to report next Monday morning so he saddled up his horse a rode the distance to Valla. There he was given a rough house built out of bush poles and hessian, the bags were painted with dry cement to make them water proof. The horses were stabled down near the horse racing track, the stables were better than his dwelling but he didn't mind as he loved his horses.

He was told that they were employing eighty men and the pay was sixteen shillings and sixpence a shift.

James had been working at the mine site for some weeks. James and his fellow workers would meet each afternoon at the hotel near the mine. The town was growing with a local bakery and grocery shop. He had become friendly with the daughter of the hotel owner of the *"Morris."* He had been discussing a venture with one of his work mates Barry Gentle who was looking at a patch of ground on the northern side of Picket Hill to grow bananas. He wanted James to join him as bananas were making good money. They both agreed the mines would not last forever.

James had received a letter from his wife that she was on her way to meet him in Sydney. She would be leaving soon from Tilbury Dock and she could not wait to see James in Sydney and her new life in NSW. The letter went on to say that her family would be at the dock to say goodbye. She went on to say that the letter was to be posted by her father.

It was a steamy morning in February 1920 as the passenger liner made its way down the Sydney Harbour and the sea gulls were putting on a grand performance. The ship was to berth at No 7 Walsh Bay. There were a number of James' old mates from the AIF there to meet their new brides. This was the last ship that the Australian Government had sponsored to bring out war brides. The ship was being manoeuvred into the wharf by two tugs. There was a party celebration mood on the wharf as the girls lined up along the rail of the ship. James was frantically looking for his Nena but he could not see her.

The ship gangplanks were lowered into place and down the passengers came. There were soldiers and ordinary passenger. James had a piece of cardboard and written on it was "Nena, welcome home."

He was still waiting there as the last of the passengers came down the gangplank. Then he heard, "Calling Mr Freeman" again and again.

Out of crowd, a member of the ship's crew came over to him. "Mr James Freeman?" he asked, looking at the sign James was holding.

"Yes, what's the problem?" asked James.

The steward started to sweat, obviously not used to the subtropical heat.

"Look I say old feller, I'm frightfully sorry, but you wife has asked me to give you this letter," he said.

James just looked at the steward and said, "But where is she? She was supposed to be on this boat. Look, I have her last correspondence, a telegram. Look here mate it reads, 'LEAVING -LONDON –TODAY- WE- WILL- BE – TOGETHER- SOON –ALL- MY- LOVE- NETA –SIGNED- LOVING- WIFE -NENA FREEMAN.'"

Then out of the crowd a lovely young girl stepped forward.

"I say Mr Freeman," she said. "I knew you wife Nena, and we worked in the same office in the East End. Look, there is only one way to say this. We docked in Cape Town and Nena did not get back on. We all had some time ashore for a look around and she just didn't return with us. I'm frightfully sorry. I know she was so looking forward to meeting your family in - where was it now – Wauchope? Hard name to say. Look, I'm sorry."

And the young lady walked off with a young man who had been standing near her.

James drifted off to the closest pub and lost himself in a few ales. He was down at the wharfs and eventually jumped on a tram and headed for George Street. He had booked into the Peoples Palace. James didn't know where the Palace was but after a few directions from passers-by, he walked up past Anthony Horden's and into Pitt Street and fronted up to his room. He fell onto the bed and cried his eyes out.

He spent the rest of the week drifting around the city and finally made his way up to Central Railway Station and boarded the North Coast Mail train. The train made its way slowly up the coast stopping at all the small and large stations and finally pulled into Pembroke at five thirty in the morning. He had not told anyone that he was returning home without his wife.

So after a couple of weeks back at the farm he decided to return to the mine.

A notice in the hotel bar read, *"Jimmy Sharman boxing troupe coming soon."* There was a rough tent out the back of the hotel and a boxing ring in the middle.

Jimmy Sharman knew James Freeman as James' cousin had fought him in a show in Wauchope. The boxing troupe was in Macksville and he promised James he would call in to Valla on their way to their next show in Coffs Harbour. They met in a pub one evening and were having a quiet drink and then it was on. Jimmy agreed to put on a show on the Wednesday night, so it was all organised.

James had arranged for three local lads to get in the ring with Jimmy's lot. Around 4pm that afternoon, someone had let the cat out of the bag, because people from all over started to pour in, the hotel was doing a roaring trade. There was mad panic as it soon became obvious that the tent area was too small. So the mine boss rigged up some more tarpaulins so if it rained it would be dry.

It was a glorious spring afternoon. Soon Jimmy had his drummer beating away Bombo, Bombo and the crowd soon got the mood of the event.

At the top of his voice, Jimmy shouted the introductions.

"Ladies and Gentlemen I have for your enjoyment this afternoon, the one and only, the North West champion all the way from Dubbo, Billy the Black Snake, never been beaten, and from Wagga Wagga, Lover Boy Brian Lane, he went all the way with Tommy Burns, and lost on a points decision. I tell you, ladies and Gentlemen, Brian will be fighting in the big tent at Rushcutters Bay soon. And last but not least, one of our boys from Kempsey, Barry Sands, Now come on fellers we are looking for three lads to see if they can go the distance. There's five quid if you are still standing after three three minute rounds. If you knock out one of my boys there will be ten quid. Come on now, let's see your stuff!"

And the drum started, Bombo, Bombo. Jimmy soon sorted out the likely lads to go in the ring. He was a fair man and he didn't want any disasters tonight and he soon picked out three likely lads. The tent was packed to capacity as the two boys entered the ring for the first bout and money was changing hands on the quiet. The first lad was a local, a returned soldier now growing beans and carrots. Valla was turning into the bean capital of NSW.

The referee entered the ring and raised Bobby Sullivan's arm.

"Ladies and Gentleman," he bellowed. "In the red corner, give him a big hand, Bobby Sullivan! And in the blue corner, Billy the Black Snake, all the way from Dubbo."

After the usual referee's messages to the fighters, he sent them back to their corners, called, "Seconds out!" and it was on.

Bobby came out with both arms flying. Billy just waited and kept him at bay and in the second round floored him and Bobby was out cold. His second threw a bucket of water over him that soon brought him around. The second fight was much closer and a young lad from Bowraville, Richard Neville a local Aboriginal had the boy from Wagga in trouble early in the first round and Jimmy was not saying much. He wanted to talk to the young lad about joining his troupe. The fight ended in a draw and young Richard walked away with five quid, very chuffed. The third fight was between another local lad from Urunga, Neville Gaddis who also went the three rounds with Brian Lane and was five quid the richer.

By ten o'clock the fighting completed. Everyone moved down to the pub.

James was having a quiet ale with Frank Atkinson, one of the miners.

"Well Jamie me lad, must be off the little lady will be waiting for me," said the miner. "I'll see you bright and early ready for work."

"Right you are Frank, see you." James had nearly finished his beer when Katherine, the young barmaid sat down beside him.

"Penny for your thoughts, James Freeman," she said. Katherine was just out from Ireland. "Aw Jamie, you look like you lost a shillin' and found thruppence."

James just looked at the young lass and France came flooding back into his head, the front and Nena, whatever went wrong.

"Let's walk, Katherine," he said. "I'll walk you back to your cabin."

The night was clear and the sky full of bright stars

"Look James, the Milky Way," said Katherine and leaned against him.

The pathway was uneven and Katherine stumbled and James caught her and caught a dizzying whiff of her perfume and for a brief moment there was stars floating around James' head. They continued past the derrick.

Then Katherine said, "Will you take me down there one day, James?"

James laughed "Ah Katherine, me dear, you wouldn't like it, its dark and spooky!"

"Ah James, me Da would take me down the pits in Dublin. I know what they're like."

James was stumped. "Well, one day I'll ask the boss."

There were a few sore heads next morning as the miners were on deck and ready to start their shift at seven thirty.

It was reported in the local press that on Tuesday the 29th of September, 1931, a tragedy occurred at the Valla Mine. It looks like the beginning of the end for the Valla Gold Mine. It has been plagued with one disaster after another.

At one thirty in the afternoon, a large stone weighing about a hundredweight fell from the roof of the workings, resulting in the death of one of the men. The remaining men walked off the site in sympathy.

It appears that at the time Mr Thomas Templeton, (shift boss) assisted by James Stanley Freeman, were engaged in timbering between the 140 ft. and 190 ft. Levels. The shift had started at the usual time of seven thirty in the morning, stopping for a lunch break at midday and resuming work at twelve thirty, when everything seemed to be quite safe. The work had proceeded for about an hour or so when, without warning a piece of rock came away from the roof and caught Freeman on the temple, felling him to the floor. The shift boss with much effort levered the stone which had been narrowly missed him and called for assistance. A stretcher was immediately sent down and the unfortunate mine worker was brought to the surface. Dr. Mulhearn of Bellingen, had been telephoned and was quickly on the spot, but found that the miner was beyond all human aid and he was pronounced dead. The Urunga Police and Bellingen Coroner were notified and arrived soon after, making the necessary arrangements for an inquiry into the circumstances attending the accident and death.

The Coroner's inquest was held at Urunga on the following Thursday at 10 am. The deceased, James Stanley Freeman served with the AIF and had a fine war record. He was well liked and known in Macksville and was a member of the Macksville Town Band. The deceased's brothers William and Leslie along with the public at large received the news with great shock when it spread through the town The remains of the deceased were buried in the Church of

England cemetery, Macksville the very Reverend G.S. Watts, who officiated at the grave side, delivered a very fine address. All the Valla Mine employees were in attendance at the graveside, James Stanley Freeman was 36y ears of age, and leaves a large circle of grieving relatives.

James Freeman served in the WW1 in the light horse in France

There was much sorrow at the Valla Mine. Morale was low after the death of James Freeman, the Valla gold mine seemed to struggle as the price of gold was depressed and the price for arsenic was low.

But in January 1932, came another blow to the mine. There was another accident involving the works manager's son Dick Shepherd. He was asphyxiated with a mixture of arsenic and cyanide. He had been working as a lab assistant when he inhaled the poisonous gas given off by the zinc box. He was rushed to Bellingen hospital. The doctors at the hospital searched information from around the world looking for a treatment but to no avail. Nothing was available to help the patient and Dick died soon after.

Despite the hard work and risks taken by miners, wages were low. Further bad news for the future came when a Roman Catholic Priest, Father Curran of Bellingen who was an eminent geologist, said that the gold content would cut out at water level but the gold would be richer than ever under the water level. Although the miners tried, they could not penetrate the water table.

The Pullun family had moved up from the Manning.

Warwicks Pullun's Grandfather had got the contract to survey and build the tram track from Pickett Hill to the Kalang River. Timber was cut and trimmed then hauled by bullock teams to the depot and loaded on the horse drawn trams which then made their way down to the Kalang River to be loaded on a paddle steamer and taken to the mill. Warwick's father then worked at the Valla Gold and Arsenic Mine.

Memory's from Warwick Pullun.

Yesterdays Memories of a kid's Golden Mine - "Those were the Days."

Valla Gold and Arsenic Mine is situated about five miles south of the village of Urunga. In its heyday, perhaps around 1921, it was equipped with a 70 horsepower boiler and winding engine air compressor, concentrating tables, roasting tables, etc. My father worked in the mine, but as a kid growing up we didn't know what a 70 horsepower boiler was and what's more, we couldn't care less.

The only time we were interested in the mine was to see Charlie Swanson at work. He had come out from Sweden and was in charge of a little stationary engine and we kids would pester him to start it up. It was fascinating to see this little engine turning a big flat belt pumping water.

We had our own business to run the business of making and having fun. Our homes were built along the main ridge that runs along from the mine to the ocean now known as Mines Road. I remember them starting at the

Ocean end. Right at the headland was Jack Marks. In a mud house next was Tom Templeton in a house made out of hessian and painted with raw cement to keep the weather out. Next was our house and iron shed. The others I remember were the Freeman's, M'Naghten's Beamish, Cooks, Whites, Prestons and others scattered around the area. Practically all of them were mine workers and families so you can see how easy it was for us kids to bunch up and have fun. One favourite way to have fun was to play in the 'White Stuff.' This, we found out later was the washings from the mined arsenic. We used to play in it up to our knees. We used to walk along McGrath's Creek with a bucket and pick passion fruit that grew wild in the gullies.

The beach was close by and we would be taken there by our parents on nice days. There were no washing machines and not much water at home so all the ladies would take their washing down to the creek and help each other till it was all done. A day at the creek was good fun for us kids.

The railway line ran close by, and our parents would take us to see the train before we went to bed. Imagine up to twenty kids singing out *"Paper! Paper!"* with all their heart and voice it was great fun. The Public School was opened in 1923 and when Warwick Pullun attended it in 1929, Mr Keating was the Principal. There were about fifteen kids in attendance. He lived in Urunga and drove to work in a brand new DeSoto. The country was in the grip of deprecation, money was short but my dad also had a DeSoto but the car went unregistered. I always remember the number plate, it was 33-031. I remember the time I got ill and Dad had to drive me to Bellingen hospital. Dad had parked in the main street and the local policeman, Sergeant Spellman glanced at the car. It didn't have rego sticker but he just looked the other way and moved on. He knew times were tough. He was what you call a good bloke.

I started my school at the Valla Mine. It was a one teacher school and the teacher's name was Mr Keating. As well as the three "Rs", we had lessons in Natural Study, Scripture and Good Manners. My wife in later years seems to think that on the latter, our teacher was a failure. The teacher had a DeSoto just like my dad's.

We started each day with prayer every morning and finished each day with a song, *'Now the Day is over.'* It was a wonderful little school. That's where I spent the happiest days of my life. If you drive over McGrath's Creek on the present Pacific Highway today, you can see a small flat on the left hand side. That's where we held our school picnics and sports, not as serious as today but more fun. There were Chaff Bag races, and three legged races, thrills and spills galore. Just imagine a play ground with no boundaries. Yes, as a kid, I reckon Valla Mines had it all. I would give my all to go back and do it all again. Because no other spot has ever replaced the hold on my affection, nor are any other incidents so clearly and tenderly etched in my memory as those days at the Valla Mine, I'm sure nothing can buy all my dreams of memories of "Arsenic and Gold."

Brian Lane had a lonely life. He was now working as a night watchmen at the Valla Gold Mine. It had virtually ceased production, there was now only a skeleton staff left, one shift with twenty miners that worked the day shift. The shops had closed, the pub was just hanging on and the publican said if business didn't pick up he would have to close.

It was Friday night and the miners couldn't work because of the flooding of the lower level. The miners were making the most of their free time and were drinking at the pub. Brian was doing his rounds. It was pitch black and he thought he heard a noise down by the main road. He wandered down to take a look as sometimes a car would break down and someone from the mine would offer help. But as he walked down past the shed a gang of three came up behind him and hit him over head, knocking him unconscious. They quickly carried him down to the main road where there was little or no traffic at this time of the day. They loaded him into their Model A Ford and took off in a northerly direction.

About a mile up the road was a turn off that led into the forest. The road was hardly ever used except for the odd kangaroo and forest worker. Alfie, one of the gang, was heading for a shed that had been used for a starting point for a timber platform to take logs down to the river. Reggie, his brother and the quiet one knew of a shed up this road he had heard about from a mate who used to drink at the 'First and Last' at the Quay at Sydney. He had a map.

After dropping Brian Lane at the shed, Billy, the third brother and supposedly the brains of the operation drove off to Urunga to phone Brian's family and tell them that he was going to hold him up for ransom.

Brian came from a prominent social family .He was the black sheep in the family and was an outcast ever since he gained employment with the NSW Correction Service back in 1936. The gang was asking for £5000. They thought Brian's family could easily afford that amount, as his brother was a member of the Bar and they were into the horse racing in a big way.

By the time Billy drove into the quiet country town of Urunga, being from Sydney he expected the town to have a public phone. He drove around for a while and finally ended up at the local hotel. Although it was 1am, there was a light in the main bar. Billy casually strolled into the bar and there was a cleaner mopping the floor.

"I say, buddy," said Billy. "Is there a public telephone box in the town?"

The cleaner looked up and said, "Gee mate, you frightened hell out of me! There's a phone box in the post office in town, it'll be open in the morning at nine."

"God, is this a hick town or what?" Billy replied and left the pub in a huff and as it was now after midnight he thought he might as well head back to the bush hut. He planned eventually to put a call into Brian's family and spill the story to the *"Truth,"* Sydney's top scandal rag, but his plans were now delayed. He skidded up to the hut and slammed to door shut, calling out so everyone could hear although there was no one in miles that could hear.

"Okay Alfie, what's to drink? Looks like we're stuck here till the post office opens in the morning." He nudged their captive on his shoulder. "Do you play cards, Brian?"

Reluctantly, Brian said, "Look, the pub in the mine will be open around six and you can get some provisions there and they have a phone."

"Bugger that," said Billy. "What privacy would we get? No, we'll just have to wait it out. But I'll drop down there later and get some Flag Ale and I think I saw a bread shop."

But the next morning, it was Alfie who drove down the bush track and called into the pub at the mine. He decided to try and ring Sydney.

"I want to make a long distant call to Sydney, how do you work the machine?" he asked Ted, the pub roustabout.

"Gee mate," said Ted. "You'll have to ring the exchange at Bellingen and put in a call. It'll cost you five bob for three minutes."

The telephone exchange at Bellingen was run by a team of four girls and they worked the day shift up until 10pm when the boys took over and did the nightshift.

Alfie lifted the receiver and a girl's voice said, "Number, please."

Miss Samantha Foster had been working at the exchange for five years and was in her last week as she was soon to be married. The operators were known as 'Hullo Girls' Samantha said again, "Number, please."

Poor Alfie was in a dither. He was not expecting to be involved in this hick town telephone talk. He was used to the big smoke.

"Ah, look it's okay love, I made a mistake, I'll ring you back later."

Although it was early in the morning he got the barman to pour him a beer. He then went over to the bakery and got hot meat pies straight out of the oven. He brought six, jumped into the car and made it back to the bush. His plan was to ring Brian Lane's home, and hold out for a ransom, and then call the *'Truth'* newspaper. This Sydney paper had all the gossip, murders, divorces, and any other raw scandals it could unearth and it came out every Sunday and was well read.

After the gang and their captive had finished the pies, Alfie decided to travel into town again and try to ring the exchange once more. This time, he was able to make a call from the phone box through the telephone exchange. But what he didn't realise was that the girl at the exchange was listening in to the call.

"Listen," he told the woman, presumably Brian's mother, when she picked up the telephone. "We've got Brian and unless you pay us £5000, you won't see him again."

"And just why should we care about that?" replied the woman with a laugh. "Go away and play, you silly little boy."

Miss Samantha Foster's fiancé belonged to the Bellingen police force. Samantha took the particulars down and traced the call to the phone box in Urunga and then called her fiancé.

"What a dimwit!" said Robert, a Senior Constable. "I'll send a car there right away."

A squad car went straight down and of course there was no one there. The officers did a search of the area and asked around. Although they were on duty, they decided to head to the Urunga pub for light lemonade. The day was stinking hot and they bar staff couldn't help them with any information but the cleaner who was off duty and having a quite beer overheard the officers talking and butted in. and told them how last night this bloke came in late wanting to make a call.

"Was he from around here?" asked the officer in charge.

"Nah, never seen him before, looked like a Sydney Slicker" replied the cleaner. "But I will say this, officer, he had a limp and a scar on his right cheek."

From behind a shed a couple of blocks away, Alfie watched the cops arrive and then go to the pub. This was all going wrong and Alfie had a bad feeling about it all. He and the other two were not used to this kind of negotiation, they were more like the 'bash 'em up or else' mob. And the woman's response to his demand had been anything but positive. He waited until the police car had driven off and then returned to the shack.

The Mulligan brothers had held Brian Lane for ten days in their makeshift goal. So it was time to act. His family didn't seem to care, their demands had not been met, and somehow, the *'Truth'* didn't want to know about it. As they drove the car back to the main road in the early hours of a Sunday morning, Brian with his hands tied behind his back, they struggled up the hill to the main shaft. At the top, the dragged Brian out of the car to the head of the shaft and without any warning they threw him into the black abyss.

Poor Brian never knew what hit him as he cascaded down to the bottom. His neck was broken as he hit the wall and by the time he reached the bottom he was dead. The brothers celebrated by finishing off a bottle of plonk and discarded the empty bottle on the edge.

Sergeant Brown from the Bellingen police had the report in front of him at the station a few hours later. He was mulling over the evidence he had before him. Then it hit him - the Mulligan Brothers. Their reputation was well known in the region. Brown had just arrived from Sydney and he had put a call into his old station at Darlinghurst and he got all the details on the brothers Alfie, Billie and Reginald. They were wanted by the Sydney Police for numerous offences. But what caught Sergeant Brown's attention was that their eldest brother, Bart was hanged in Darlinghurst goal in the late 30s.

The Bellingen exchange also recorded a call to a phone number in Bondi, to a Mrs Brian Lane, the wife of the last hangman in NSW. His last hanging was one of the Mulligan brothers Bart. It didn't take long for the local police to trace Barry Lane's last known address, which was the Valla Gold Mine.

The police put out a general alert to be on the lookout for a green Model A Ford. The police arrived soon after at the mine with all horns blazing The Mine manager escorted them to the night watchman's apartment. It was locked and they could not raise any one inside the hut. The police were starting to get nervous they explained to the manager what they thought was on with the Mulligan Brothers. They interviewed the publican and barman and they were told that a shady looking character had turned up and tried to phone Sydney. It didn't take long before a group of workers was rallied to check out the area and last they checked out the shafts. There was no evidence of any foul play with number 1 or number 2 shafts but when they shone a torch down shaft number 3, there at the bottom was a body. Two of the miners were lowered down and called out that there was a body and it was Brian Lane. They sent down a cradle and lifted the body up to the surface.

The body was soon confirmed as Brian Lane. Brian had retired from the Judiciary as the last hangman in NSW. His last hanging was Bart Mulligan, a member of the Mulligan gang that had terrorised the Kings Cross area.

A quick examination of the body's location in the shaft indicated that the body must have been thrown from the head of the shaft and the police car headed there at once. The empty bottle was immediately spotted and wrapped up for inspection and several footprints showed several men had been there.

Alfie and his brothers fronted the Nambucca Hotel in Macksville wanting a room. Unknown to them, there had been a flood in Kempsey which had closed the highway. So the lads settled in for the night drinking at the bar. Reggie was soon half asleep. Alfie just looked at him and got his brother to escort him up the stairs to sleep it off.

The river that runs through Kempsey had cut the main highway north, meaning no traffic could go north or south. The barman told the boys that they would have to travel to Bowraville and then cut through to Bellingen and up to Dorrigo and then on to Armidale and onto Sydney, if they were lucky. It was early next morning when the brothers set off on this mad journey. Although the Model A was sturdy, it was not fitted out for cross country travel over rough back country.

As they drove down the main street of Bowraville, Billie said, "Look boys, a pub! Let's have a drink."

Alfie looked back at his brother and said, 'Fair Dinkum, Billie! We have just thrown a bloke down a pit and killed him. The fuzz will be onto us quick time. No, we must push on."

Alfie was correct. The police had been checking all the hotels in the area, aware that the main highway was closed because of local flooding. When Sergeant Brown who had been put in charge of the man hunt reached the hotel in Macksville it did not take them long to find out that the Mulligans had stayed and were trying to get around the flooded roads by tracking over Bowraville and onto Bellingen. There was only one way through that country and they would get a road block set up at a place called Briarfield. He quickly put a call into his station and got a promise of immediate action.

"They won't get past us," said the Sergeant. "They might know the back streets of Sydney but this is the bush."

The brothers had turned down into Missabotti. A fog had sprung up, thick as pea soup and they were reduced to a crawl, so it was past midnight when they finally realised they had missed the turn. Another hundred yards along, they came to a forest gate.

"Bloody Hell!" shouted Alfie "Reggie you were reading the mud map!"

They drove back along the dirt track until they came to a junction and the sign indicated twelve miles to Bellingen. It was now in the early morning and visibility was down to a few feet. Then all of a sudden, another problem arose.

"What the heck?" Alfie cried out as they came to a milk truck stopped right in the middle of the road.

Alfie got out of the car and said, "I say mate any chance of shifting this excuse for a wagon?"

Barry Stewart was just starting his milk round. He collected milk from all the outlying properties and today he had a problem. He was not in the mood for this carry on.

"What's your problem? He snapped. "Look, I've got a flat and I'm due for my first milk pick up in thirty minutes."

So there was nothing the brothers could do but to help him change the tyre and put the spare on. As the last nut was tightened, the boys jumped back in in the car and were away.

"What else can go wrong?" shouted Reggie they drove on without any further incident. He got no reply. A few minutes later, he spoke again.

"Briarfield coming up," he said. "There's a junction, we take the left hand turn and it's only a few miles to the next town."

Ernie Graham drove the school bus run from Bellingen through Briarfield down South Bank Road and home to Hungry Head. He was on an early run to start his pick up for the school run. When he got to the intersection of the Bowraville road, he couldn't believe his eyes. There was a police car blocking the road.

Ernie got down from the bus and said, "What's going on Sergeant?"

"Ernie, you can't go on this morning" replied the officer. "I'll get you to park the bus over there and stay inside, could be some fireworks soon."

It wasn't long before the green Model A appeared around the corner. The road had improved since the gang had left Missabotti and they were hurtling along at sixty miles an hour. But Reggie, who was now driving, put it into a skid and came to a broadside fifty yards from the police barricade.

"The game's up fellers, we know who you are, so leave the car with your hands in the air, nice and slow," called the sergeant, using a megaphone.

At first the boys just froze. Reggie started to open the door but Alfie said, "Close the door you fool, we're going to make a run for it."

At first, the sergeant just looked and said to the officers, "This won't take long. They can't get past Thora, the river is in flood they're bloody fools."

But then the unexpected happened. The Ford lunged forward, side-swiped the school bus and roared down the road towards Bellingen. Shaking his head at the stupidity of the gang, the sergeant ordered his officers into the car and they took off in pursuit. It didn't last long. As the chase passed the turn off into the hospital, a garbage truck was coming out and the Ford crashed straight into it.

When the police officers got out and walked to the crash site, the Mulligan brothers were lying unconscious in the car. One had a split head and looked in a bad way. Sergeant Brown got onto things quickly and had back up to cordon off the road. Hospital staff were quickly on the scene, mainly to see the drama unfold but they had stretchers on the spot and with the police force help had the three brothers into the hospital emergency ward.

It didn't take long for a member of the press to get on the scene. Barry Dark from the local paper, the Bellingen Sun, along with half the local town was causing a traffic jam. The local school bus driver soon continued on his way and would have great stories to tell the students.

Barry Stewart drove past half an hour later and continued to pick up milk cans. He stopped at the police van and called out to Sergeant Brown.

"Hey, Ted, are we still on for bowls this afternoon?"

The local newspaper had a telegram for the *Truth* newspaper in Sydney. The editors wanted a full report. A further telegram read, *"Can you meet train tomorrow morning we have a photographer and Journalist departing Sydney this afternoon arrive Raleigh tomorrow morning. We would like shots of the Valla Mine etc. we are sending Peter Stevenson."*

The mail train arrived on time at 6.35 am. Barry was given the job of picking up the journo and cameraman.

"Gee, you got some gear," said Barry.

"Oh well, you never can tell," replied one. "I'm Peter Stevenson and this is Mike Smith."

Barry loaded the gear into the wagon and took off down the Hwy to Hungry Head.

"Barry, any chance of a feed?" asked Stevenson. "We're starving! Bloody hell, no breakfast till we pulled into Kempsey, then only weak coffee and a meat pie."

"Don't worry boys," replied the milkman. "I know the kitchen staff at the Urunga pub, best meal on the coast."

Later, as the newspapermen gorged themselves on bacon and eggs and a pile of toast you couldn't jump over, Barry explained that he had a chance to get one of the Mulligan boys to talk and he spilled the beans about a shed where they had been holed up for ten days.

"Let's go!" exclaimed Stevenson. "As soon as we've finished this lot!"

A couple of hours later, they reached the mine site and were shown the shaft. The cameraman took photos while the journo went off to talk to the hotel staff.

Stevenson then wanted to look at the bush hut, so one of the miners volunteered to guide them out to the forest. The shed was in a mess. The Mulligans had left it in a state. Although they were there for only a short time, the place was littered with grog bottles and newspapers. The newspapermen and their guide made their way back to the mines hotel and got roaring drunk. Poor Barry from the Bellingen Sun was in no shape to go back to work so he led the Sydney newspaper men back to Raleigh railway station and let them wait for the afternoon train. The following Sunday the Truth paper was front page and every one in NSW knew where Valla was.

On the next Sunday, just like any Sunday afternoon at the Sydney Domain, speakers gathered and stood on their soap boxes and spoke about all and sundry. They spoke about Religion, the end of the world, Jesus is coming and he is not happy. They spoke about politics and how the communist were always there.

A young barrister who had just entered politics for the conservatives had just made his opening remarks when from the back of the crowd, a voice a lady called out, "What about 'ousing what are you going to do about that?"

"Well madam, the first thing we will do is put an "H" in it," replied the barrister.

There was a roar from the crowd. and then there was A.V. Kay who usually spoke on any and all subjects.

"Today ladies and gentleman I want to speak on the subject of capital punishment," he began. "This week on our north coast, the life of a brave Australian Mr Brian Lane was snuffed out. For those who don't remember him, he was our hangman and he put to death a member of the Mulligan gang. Now the Mulligan gang have been brought back to Sydney and will face trial and will get jail sentences when they should be hung up!"

There was another roar from the crowd, from both opponents of capital punishment and those for it. The police were on standby as there was always trouble when the subject of capital punishment came up. Then it was on, man and women, for and against, it was becoming a battle then the police in the Black Marias came roaring in and arrests were made.

An Abandoned Relic.

The Valla mine area was becoming a danger to the public so over the next few years, the shafts were closed off and filled in. In 1980 all traces of the mine area were cleared

So ended the story of the Valla Gold mine and the hopes of many prospectors who sought riches and those, more mundane, who sought employment, especially during the depression years.

Madonna

Our trip to Belgium

In September 2011, my wife and I spent some time in Belgium.

We devoted a day to Waterloo and visited the battle grounds of the famous Battle of Waterloo. It is amazing that the battle was all over in 24 hours, The Little General had turfed out a farmer and used this residence as his command post. The day before the battle, both sides had a meeting on how and when the war would start.

The casualties on the day were huge on the British side under Wellington. They were reported to have lost 22,000, including British, Dutch, German and Prussians. The French causalities were 25,000 dead and 8,000 were taken prisoners. The loss of horses would have been huge.

We also visited the war graves at Tyne Cott and Wipers or (Ypres).

But the highlight of the day was attending the ceremony at the Menin Gate, where over the last 80 years except during WW2, the local fire brigade has performed the Last Post at 8pm each night. This night there were over 500 people there and for an Australian, it was very moving (not a dry eye in the group).

The next day we went on to Bruges, sometimes called the Venice of the North. Bruges has many highlights but none can surpass the statue of Madonna. Michelangelo sculpted the statue out of marble between 1501 to 1504 and the Madonna and Child is located in *"Onze Lieve Vrouwekerk."*

The work is also notable in that it was the only sculpture to leave Italy during the artist's lifetime. It was bought by Giovanni and Alessandro Moscheroni (Mouscron) from a family of wealthy cloth merchants in

Bruges, then one of the leading commercial cities in Europe. The sculpture was sold for 4,000 florins.

When our group was looking in the church, there was a guard on duty in a brown uniform ensuring that no photos were taken. He reminded me of Hitler's Brown Shirts.

The sculpture was removed twice from Belgium after its initial arrival. The first was in 1794, after French Revolutionaries had conquered the Austrian Netherlands during the French Revolutionary Wars. The citizens of Bruges were ordered to ship it and several other valuable

works of art to Paris. It was returned after Napoleon's final defeat at Waterloo in 1815.

The second removal was in 1944, during World War II, with the retreat of German soldiers who smuggled the sculpture to Germany enveloped in mattresses in a Red Cross truck. It was found two years later in Altaussee/ Austria and again returned. It now sits in the Church of Our Lady in Bruges, Belgium. [3]

---

[3] *We had just seen the movie "The Monument Men" which is based on the taking of the statue and many other famous pieces of art.*

God, I Hate the Cold!

In May 2007, my wife and I set out from Sydney to fly around the world. We were to attend my wife's nephew's wedding in South Africa.

When the plane landed in Jo'burg, they had experienced snow for the first time in thirty years. To cut a long story short, we flew to Cape Town, boarded a ship to the Island of St Helena (to research and photos for my first book, *"Curse the Bells")* then back to Walvis Bay in Botswana then back to Jo'Burg. We were off to a Safari park called Makutsi, a five hour journey from Jo'burg.

Finally we arrived, late in the afternoon and were escorted to our rondavel. The park was completely enclosed and the wild animals, including the Big Five roamed throughout the 500-odd acres. So you did not venture out after dark. You could walk down to the breakfast canteen in the morning, you could roam around keeping within the immediate complex and as long as you returned to your cabin before dark, you were safe, I think.

We were venturing out one morning, it was the seventh of July, to tour the park and see the wild life. We were picked up at around 5am and it was damn cold, the vehicle was an open Land Cruiser. We had befriended a young couple from Tasmania, Sue, Millie (twelve months old), Grant and Oscar, nine were sitting at the back and Laura ten. God, they were from Australia! Most of the other guests were from Germany.

As we ventured into the unknown it was bloody cold - beanies blankets and gloves and we were still freezing. Elizabeth and I were in the second tier, Sue and Millie next to the driver.

God, I Hate the Cold!

We had been gone about thirty minutes and all I could feel was I would prefer to be back in bed. When all of a sudden, our driver said, "Lion!" and in the early morning mist the big cat just got up and strolled off. Our driver could see six in total.

He said, "I know where going to, there's a water hole not far from here."

So off we went down this track and lo and behold, there they were six of them. But they did not stop to drink but kept on coming up the track towards us. My wife later said she could have reached out and touched one of them as it passed. Somehow it didn't seem to be as cold as before. The rule is no talking or standing, the animals are accustomed to the vehicle. The management was not happy about allowing young children on these trips as they could cause the

animals to panic. But Millie was perfect and some years later she said to her mother something about "Big Cat Diaries" and how it reminded her of the trip.

It was good to be back for breakfast and hot coffee.

I hate the cold.

Admiralty House.

Admiralty House was built in the early 1800s and called Wotonga as a private residence and finally used from 1885-1935 by the Royal Navy.

Admiralty House in Sydney is the Sydney residence of the Governor General of Australia. I worked there in the 1950s as a junior gardener. My mother was related to Sir William McKell and my great-grandmother was his aunt.

My first introduction to Admiralty house was at a fete held for the cubs and scouts of Sydney. The residence has been open to charities up until 2000 for garden fetes. I never realized that I would return there in the 1950s as a gardener.

The Governor General was Sir William Slim and he and Lady Slim had just arrived from India where he was the Viceroy, and Lady Slim wanted all the palm trees removed because they reminded her of her time in India. She did not get all her own way, as our head gardener, George Gilliam refused to allow that to happen.

I enjoyed my time as a gardener there. There were many celebrities that visited Admiralty house, including Danny Kay, and there were always delegations from various governors and ambassadors from overseas. As a junior gardener, one of my jobs, included raking the huge driveway every day and each day, one of the juniors would drive to McMahon's point to collect lunches and lottery tickets. On one occasion, I came back with a ticket which I had called 'Lady Slim.' My gardener Bruce was horrified and he said that we would be charged for defamation of character.

"Bruce," I said. "If we win the lottery, Lady Slim can go and jump."

One morning I arrived for work and there in front of us was the Dee Why ferry from Manly. In a heavy fog, it had crashed into the point. We also saw the flying boats leaving Rose Bay and many a day we would see warships come and go. It was a sad day when we saw the Voyager coming through the heads making its way down the Harbour into Garden Island, its front all smashed in. It was a terrible day for the Australian Navy.

The Manly Ferry rams into Admiralty House in fog

The old hands would tell stories of past GGs and they liked to tell me about McKell, how he would go around and collect all the soap and take it back to Canberra. It was his Labor values coming through.

Kirribilli House was next door. It was built in 1854 for a merchant, Adolphus Frederic Feez for the purchase price of two hundred pounds.

Admiralty House

The grand structure had fallen into disrepair, as it had not been used for some time. While I was there, it was renovated and it was to be used to house the Prime Minister when in Sydney and its first resident was the Prime Minister Robert Gordon Menzies.

Popskie's Private Army

Popskie was born in Belgium in 1897 to Russian-Jewish intellectual parents. The private army was a unit in the British Special forces founded in Cairo in December 1942 by Lieutenant Vladimir Peniakoff, DSM MC (Popskie)

Popskie's Private Army went to war to seek out and harass and attack Field Marshal Rommel's fuel supplies. It was disbanded in Italy in September 1945.

When the Second World War broke out, after he was rejected by the Royal Air Force and Royal Navy, Popskie was reluctantly taken on by the British Army who assigned the middle-aged Belgian to mundane garrison duties as an Arabic-speaking junior officer in the Libyan Arab Force (LAF).

Popskie plotted his escape and formed the Libyan Arab Force Commandos – a small group of British and Libyan soldiers who operated behind the lines in the Jabel Akhdar area, Cyenaica.

After returning to Cairo, he was invited to join the Long Range Desert Group (LRDG) and lost his little finger to an Italian bullet and received the Military Cross.

It was shortly after this that the PPA was formed, the smallest independent unit of the British Army, just twenty-three men of all ranks. The original officers of the PPA had served together in the LAF. These were Popski, Robert Park, Yunnie and Jean Caneri.

Events proceeded rapidly as the Germans and Italians were chased out of North Africa almost before the PPA had got started. A joint PPA and LRDG patrol discovered a gap in the mountains that let Montgomery's armour outflank Rommel's defence.

PPA was among the first elements of the 8th army pushing west to meet up with the British 1st army and American 2nd Corps. Pushing east in Tunisia in early 1943, many PPA raiding and reconnaissance operations were carried out around the time of the Kasserine Pass fighting, including the surrender of 600 Italians to British and American forces.

At first the wireless operators had trouble getting their tongues around Peniakoff so it was shortened to Popski.

PPA used lightly armoured special jeeps equipped with 303 calibre Vickers and 50 calibre Browning machine guns which were essential for their long range speed and firepower.

Captain Brian Ewart Thomas who was a member of the P.P.A. died 3rd June 2014 two weeks before his 91st birthday. At the age of 22 he was responsible for his most famous exploit. He was tasked with bringing six of Popskie's jeeps across the Lido of Venice to land them at St Marks Square just before the surrender of the German forces in Italy. This achievement of Popskie was ambitious and astonished the locals, as no wheeled vehicle had ever been there before or indeed since.

Mist In the Valley

Does the mist still drift
Through the valleys
Like it did when I was there?

Does the smell of leaves and seaweed
Still linger in the air
Is Valla's dear old Deep Creek
Still flowing out to sea?

Is the Valley still as beautiful
As it used to look to me?

Do the colours of the mountains
Still change from day to day?

Is the river still as clear
As it was before I went away?

Does the morning sun on the ocean
Still sparkle like a gem?

Are the people still as kind
As I remember them?

By Robyn T.

Valla Flats

The old Pacific Highway crossed the main railway line at the Nambucca Railway station and wound its way through green hills, past Cow Creek and down through Frogs Hollow, there was a mist on Mount England, finally up and over the hill and down into Deep Creek. On the left was 'Deep Creek Used Cars' and on the right was Deep Creek Caravan Park and General Store. It was a meeting place for locals to gather and spread stories and discuss prices of beans. Valla was the Bean Capital of Australia during the Second World War. Beans were picked up by Lindsay brothers Transport and taken to Sydney markets.

A local resident, John along with his mate Bill had arrived and were having a coffee with the garage owner, Bernie. They were having a great chinwag about Australia becoming a republic. John and Bernie were loyal to the Queen and Bill was all for a republic.

It was a fine weekend and Jock was holding a garage sale and general auction. John and Bill were well known for bidding against each other. On one sale, John got lumbered with a cardboard box full of girls' marching uniforms. So John got the name of Hong Kong John. Not to be outdone, throughout the Valley Bill was known as Bullshit Bill.

The sale was typical of Deep Creek sales, full of junk, but at the end of it, Jock would have a pocket full of notes. He was a crafty old Scottish character. Everybody would end up across at the cafe for coffee and steak sandwiches. Anne was a great cook and nobody went away hungry.

John was looking for a new set of wheels so he went back across the road with Bill, dodging trucks.

"Jock," he said. "What have you got regarding a car, registered and in good condition?"

Jock led them down through the rubbish and derelict cars that had seen better days.

"John, I can let you have this beauty for \$500," he said. "The rego's just run out but I know somebody can let you have a pink slip, no trouble. It goes real well and it's got a firkin' good motor."

"Thanks Jock," replied John. "I'll give it a miss, thanks all the same."

With that, Bill and John wandered off back to Bill's Shed for more coffee and a yarn.

The Adventures of Chris

Roma pulled up at the Tamworth bus stop to pick up her grandson Chris who was a descendant of John Joseph Layburn. Chris had phoned and said he had had enough at his mother's place. He never wanted to see his mother again. His parents had been divorced for some time and Chris had stayed at his Nanna's place six years before. He was now eighteen and considered himself an adult.

The bus pulled up, right on time. There he was, all smiles, curly hair, the bottoms of his jeans dragging in the dirt around his ankles, red shirt and a big black hat, runners that looked like they came from the tip; all his belongings in a stripy bag. He threw it in the back of the Ute. "Got a fag, Nanna?"

"Thought you were giving them up," she said as she coughed. Roma had been trying to give them up for the last forty years.

"I've tried the patches but they don't work," said Chris.

Roma had to drive through the Manilla Township, which was halfway to Barraba. Clouds were gathering out in the west.

"The sky looks like it might rain, Nanna," said Chris.

"I doubt it," replied Roma.

Arthur and Roma had been in Barraba for twenty years and she'd had enough. She hated the place, cold in winter and hot in summer. This year had been the worst drought on record. As they crossed the Manilla River, which was now a series of water holes, a flock of magpies flew past the Ute.

"Bastards!" she said.

Birds weren't Roma's best friends; they were always messing up her washing line. Roma pulled into the main street of Barraba to get her supplies bread, milk and of course, fags.

Chris had spent one year at Barraba primary schools in the early 90s. Walking down the dusty, deserted street, he bumped into one of his old school mates sauntering along listening to music on his walkman.

"Nathan, how are you?" Chris said.

They discussed the latest 'Eminem' CD.

"Are you working, Nathan?"

"Nar, on the dole," said young Nathan. "No work around here, things are tough, had a couple of days two months ago at Bongala but nothing since. I have an uncle down at Coffs Harbour, works on a trawler, reckons he can get me a job, but they want you to work nights and weekends and I would probably get seasick."

"I worked on a trawler at Forster last summer," Chris replied. "Good money but the work ran out."

"There's a party Saturday night, Chris," said Nathan. "Do you want to come?"

"I don't know," replied Chris. "I'm supposed to go to work at my aunt's place. Her boss may have some work for me, at Bingala, but I'll be at my Nanna's place for a while."

The discussion had to end as Roma struggled out of the shop, laden with supplies, mostly dog food. Roma and Arthur had fifteen working dogs and loved every one of them. Arthur would tell any interested listener that they were all working dogs.

The road out to Horton Falls was now mostly bitumen, the result of a bi-centenary grant back in 1988, but the last six kilometres was still dirt and it turned into a quagmire when it rained. Reaching the turn-off to the property, Roma drove up to the gate where they were met by Trixy, an Australian terrier, with two puppies at her side. Chris walked up to the cottage standing starkly amongst the dry, hungry countryside surrounded by boulders and tufts of grass.

Sally, the Australian stock horse, now blind in both eyes, came up to meet the group. The horse knew Roma's voice and nuzzled her hand for a sweet. Roma knew that the day was coming when she would have to make the decision to have her beloved horse put down, but she continued to resist the idea as she loved her twenty-year-old horse. Chris helped Roma carry the supplies into the house.

"Put the kettle on please, Art," said Roma.

"Did you get the Bysol, Roma?" Art called out.

"Nar, Barry said it won't be in till next week."

Art worked around the properties doing shearing and stock work. In addition, he sometimes did panel beating at the local garage. The drought was having a big effect on his income, and these odd jobs helped pay the bills.

"Art, what did Jan say about Chris working at Bingala?" asked Roma.

"She said for him to come out Monday," said Art. "I could be fencing out there next week, so I'll drop him out."

"How much will she pay?"

Chris chimed in. "Don't be cheeky. You should be thankful for the work."

"I don't do charity work, you know," snapped Roma.

Chris could see Roma starting to get her Irish temper up.

"Look, Chris, I don't want you hanging around town," said Roma. "Keep away from the pubs. They're a bad lot in there."

"Nathan said there's a party in town Saturday night," said Chris.

"Where will you stay? No, Chris, stay here this weekend, Art wants you to help clean up the place, please."

Chris had always been a bit of a bugger. Using his charm and good looks, he gained popularity with the girls at school and won over the female teachers. His father loved telling the story of how Chris had driven his infant school teacher to distraction. One particular day, the teacher angrily told the errant lad she could kill him. In the afternoon, she gently touched his shoulder and told him she had not meant it.

With a big cheeky grin that stretched from ear to ear, Chris turned his big blue eyes to her and said, "I knew you were only kidding."

Chris walked down to the gate. He was not happy. The argument with his mother had been about her selling his skateboard. He strolled down the dirt track with Rex by his side, the male Australian terrier that had fathered most of the dogs on the place. They reckoned he would have to stand on a box to service the bigger dogs. Sighting a lone rabbit, the old dog chased the hapless creature into the scrub. Rabbits were scarce these days. Art said something about calicivirus being the reason for their disappearance.

Chris had walked about five hundred metres down the road when suddenly three big kangaroos hopped across the road. Just as he turned around to walk back, an old Holden pulled up beside him, driven by a stranger.

"Want a lift?" she asked.

Chris peered into the driver's window.

'Not bad, but a bit old,' he thought to himself. *'She must be at least thirty.'*

"Thanks," he said.

"You're not from around here, Curley? Michelle's the name," the woman said

"No, I am staying at my Nanna's place, 'White Hut.'"

"Art and Roma's place?" Michelle said.

"Yeah, I've come up to look for some work," he replied as he opened the door and slid in beside her.

She drove into White Hut and stopped outside the house.

Roma came to the door. "Cuppa tea?"

"Thanks, Roma, just met this young spunk down the road."

Michelle with her husband had a hundred acres of sparsely vegetated goat country near Horton Falls. The couple had moved from the city after the information technology firm for whom her husband worked downsized the workforce. The large redundancy payout supported their current feral lifestyle. Their house was not much to look at, but it was comfortable in the summer. They skinny-dipped in the creek with their only daughter, Samantha, who was in her last year at high school. Like most of the smart local kids, she wanted to go to Sydney University to gain a degree and escape from the bush.

"Chris, will you help feed the dogs?" Roma called from the feed shed. Opening the drum, she was startled by a huge rat that scurried out into the paddock. The half-blind terrier raced after it. Roma's youngest son Steven, who was living down the coast, had left his dog, a Tenterfield terrier called Ben, on the property. Everyone reckoned the dog was really a Jack Russell because of the dog's skill at catching rodents. Barking with delight, the excited dog disturbed a flock of black and white Choughs feeding on the ground below the peppercorn tree.

Eventually Ben caught the rat down by the small dam. Chris, Art and Michelle had drunk two cups of tea when Roma came through the wire door. She realized that in her hurry at the shops, she had not bought enough cigarettes for the weekend.

"Art, are you going into town tomorrow?" she asked.

"Why?" he said.

"Oh Art, I'll run out of fags before Sunday."

Art had started to put his foot down and now refused to buy any for her. She did not look well, their doctor had advised her to stop smoking but he might as well have talked to a brick wall.

"I'll get them for you, Roma," Michelle said.

"Thanks a lot," Roma replied as she gave Art a dirty look.

"Brian and I have to go into town in the morning." Chris butted in. "Can I come with you, Michelle?"

"Yes, we will be going early, 7 am, meet us at the gate."

Roma thought to herself, *'I wonder why they are going at that hour?'*

Chris retired early to his room with his earphones and his latest CD.

Roma knocked on his door about 11 pm.

"Go to sleep, Chris, you have to be up early to meet the Mulligans if you want to go into town."

As Roma walked to her bedroom, she muttered to herself that she would never get the place cleaned up.

Next morning, as he waited for the Mulligan's, Chris ate a piece of toast. Although it was early spring, there was a nip in the air and a touch of frost on the ground. Brian pulled up in a dirty, dusty old car. As Chris climbed into the back seat, he noticed the words 'wash me' written on the back window. Brian introduced their pretty daughter Samantha to the blond haired city lad. Chris was starting to think that this was going to be a great few weeks.

"Call me Sam," she said.

Chris had no trouble chatting with Sam about life in Barraba. He was surprised that he knew some of the old school friends Sam mentioned.

Michelle turned around and said, "Chris, we have to go to Manilla to pick up some things, we'll be back through Barraba around noon, meet us outside the pub in the centre of town."

"I won't go with you, Mum, I'll show Chris around town," replied Sam.

"That won't take long," Brian remarked.

Sam and Chris started to walk down to the main part of town.

"Bit early, isn't it? What do your Mum and Dad have to go to Manilla for?" queried Chris.

"To pick up stuff," remarked Sam.

"What are we going to do?" Chris thought it was a bit early for the pub, anyhow he was broke.

"Don't worry, we will go around to my friend Lauren's place, at least we can have a cup of coffee."

They walked through the gate and up the front steps. Old Mr Suffolk was in his chair drinking coffee and having his first fag of the day. He looked awful. Mr Norman

Suffolk had never worked since they closed down the asbestos mine at Woods Reef back in the 80s.

"Morning, Mr Suffolk," Sam said.

"Who's that?" the old man asked, looking up from the paper he was trying to read.

Samantha was obviously a good friend, as she walked uninvited into the house headed for Lauren's bedroom. Knowing her, she would probably be still in bed.

The young couple walked down the hall. The place was a mess.

Norm's wife had run off ten years before, and left him to bring up his two daughters. Lauren's older sister had moved to Sydney twelve months ago. He had not heard from her since she left, but one of Lauren's girlfriends at school told her that she had heard that she was on the game at the Cross.

The door to Lauren's room was wide open and they barged in. "Wake up, wake up!" Sam said.

"Christ, what time is it? Sam, make me a coffee please. Wow! Who have we here?"

"Chris, I would you like to meet Lauren," Sam said as she walked into the kitchen to make the coffee. Since Lauren's sister had left, she was the cook and housemaid. Her father was now going to AA meetings and was off the grog. Mind you, he had tried before, but he had promised his daughter this time he meant it. He had even started helping out at the Salvos opportunity shop where he had met a lonely widow of his own age called Doris. He kept telling himself it would give him something to do. He was sick of watching TV through the day.

Sam came back to the bedroom door. "Sure you don't want a cuppa, Chris?" she asked.

"OK, milk and two sugars please," he said.

Lauren sleepily sat up, not noticing that the front of her silk pyjamas was gaping, revealing a firm, beautiful young body. Chris, who was sitting on the bed, could not take his eyes off her.

Sam came back with a tray and placed it on the table.

Lauren was sixteen and in her fourth year at high school. She wanted to be a vet; it was a very demanding programme requiring higher marks than medicine. Lauren broke the silence.

"Are you going to Nat's party tonight?"

Chris went on to explain how he had to be back to help Art that afternoon and be ready to go to Bingala on Monday.

Sam chimed in, "I don't think Mum and Dad will be back today."

"But they said they would pick us up at the pub at lunch time," said Chris.

Lauren laughed and Sam joined in, "Maybe they will or maybe they won't."

"What's that supposed to mean?" Chris asked.

"They get together with their friends and they party," said Sam.

"But it's Saturday morning," he said.

"Anyway Chris," said Lauren, "if you want to ring Roma and tell her, it will be OK for you and Sam to stay here. We have spare beds, it's cool." With that, Lauren got out of bed and got dressed, ignoring Chris' fascinated stares.

When they got back downstairs, Chris tried to ring Roma and after the third try, he got through to her.

"Nanna, it's Chris. Michelle and Brian haven't turned up, can I stay here and we'll come home in the morning?"

"You little shit! Who's we?" Roma was furious. She had been trying to clean up the place for months, junk and old cars were lying around. She dreamed of moving to the coast; anywhere it was warm.

Chris continued trying to get a word in. "Sam is with me. We are going to stay at her friend Lauren's place."

"Is that Norman Suffolk's place?"

"Yes, Nanna."

"That's OK then, behave. Art will be in tomorrow, don't move from there. He will pick you up!"

The girls decided to go out to eat. Chris still had on his jeans, red shirt and black cowboy hat; Roma reckoned he slept in it.

Lauren whispered to Sam, "Sexy, isn't he?"

They ordered a pizza from Bev's Takeaway. Chris protested the whole time that he was broke. They sat at the outside table, ate the pizza and drank coke. Some of the girls' school friends passed by wanting to join in, keen to meet the new boy in town with the big black hat.

As the party did not start until 10 pm, they walked back to Lauren's place to watch TV.

That night, Nathan met them at the door. It was early, but young people were already dancing on the front veranda. His parents had gone with friends to play the pokies at the RSL. The music was loud; the police had already been around to give them a warning. The local sergeant knew that Nathan was overall a good kid, but at the first sign of drugs or excessive alcohol, he would come down on them like a ton of bricks.

On his second visit, the sergeant asked young Chris his name and how long he had been in Barraba.

Lauren sprang to his defence.

"Sarge, he's staying with his nanna Roma, and Art, out at White Hut on Horton Falls Rd."

This seemed to satisfy the cop, but he said at the last moment, "OK, son, but keep out of trouble, I know where you live."

Chris was about to say, 'What's that supposed to mean?' but thought better of it.

The party went well into the night. Finally, around 2 am, they decided to leave and Chris was reasonably sober. Sam was drunk. It was not far to Lauren's place and as they walked up the path, the front door was wide open. In a country town like Barraba the place was never locked. Old Norm had said he had nothing worth stealing. They struggled down the hallway and helped Sam onto the bed in the spare room. She was out cold.

"Where do you want me to sleep, Lauren?" Chris asked.

Lauren looked at him and held out her hand. She drew him into her room. Chris undressed down to his jocks.

"Be back in a moment," she said. "I'll go and see if the old man's asleep."

Chris got under the sheets. Lauren came back into the room.

"He must be staying over at his friend's place tonight, the old devil. Since he has stopped drinking, he's got a sparkle in his eye again."

Chris was not sure what was going to happen, so he just lay there with his back to the wall. She snuggled into him and went to sleep. Lauren woke first and her hands started to wander over his muscular, brown body. Chris slowly woke and turned to her. She started to kiss him passionately, stroking him all over. Just as she was about to climb on top of him, Sam came through the door and asked, "What's for breakfast?"

Chris, deeply embarrassed, sat up and tried to get out of bed but Lauren dragged him back down.

"It's OK, there's no rush," said Sam and closed the door.

Lauren got up, put on a dressing gown and went to talk to Sam in the kitchen.

"Sam, give us fifteen minutes, will you?" she asked and returned to the bedroom. A triumphant Lauren and a very satisfied Chris came out again about half an hour later.

Art pulled up about 10 am. Chris and Sam climbed into his truck and drove back to White Hut. Samantha did not have a clue where her parents had got to, but she was used to them going off. Art offered to drive her home but she said she would walk as she was used to it.

Chris helped Art load the truck as they were leaving early in the morning. As Art drove the truck down the track in the early morning mist, he waved to Roma. There was a cool breeze coming off Mount Kaputar and it made Art shiver. The cold weather made his back ache. Deep down, he wanted to move to the coast, but with the drought and low land prices, nobody wanted to buy White Hut. However, Brian reckoned he knew some mates in Sydney who could be interested in purchasing a western property. These potential buyers had benefited from the escalating Sydney property prices and had substantial funds to invest. Just a matter of waiting!

The road to Bingala was gravel and badly rutted, as the council grader had not graded the road for some months. Chris broke the silence. "The road's bloody bad." There was an uncomfortable silence. Art never said much. He would much rather be playing tennis. Since his joints began giving him hell, all he really wanted to do was move out of Barraba to the coast.

The truck crossed the dried creek bed as sheep strolled out of their path. Chris got out, opened the gate and walked in to meet his Auntie Jan, who said, "I've got the kettle on."

Chris grabbed his stripy bag and threw it into the spare bedroom.

"Art, the boss wants you to take Chris down to the western paddock to start on the fence," said Jan. "Anyway, come in and have something to eat first."

Chris was going to board the train at Bingala, as it was forty kilometres back to Art's place.

"What's the pay like, Aunt?"

"The boss said he wants you for three weeks at $400 per week less tax, take it or leave it, and board." His aunt was renowned for not holding things back.

They drove over the paddocks, through three sets of gates. Art knew his fencing and he soon had Chris digging postholes. They had one kilometre of fencing to replace the temporary fence that had been hastily erected after the last big wet. Bingala was a large property of 20,000 acres, stocked with beef and sheep. It even included a landing strip which was multipurpose. The owners of the property would fly into Armidale or Tamworth to do the shopping.

On her rounds, Jan checked the water troughs and stock and took the boys their lunch as they were working some distance from the homestead. The boys returned to Art's place on Friday afternoon.

Although Chris's hands were cut and sore from handling the barbwire, the next day he helped Art load up the truck with a load of junk. Art promised to drop Chris at Lauren's place when he went in to the tip.

Chris had spruced himself up. Roma had washed his good jeans and that red shirt; he was looking forward to catching up with Lauren. Chris liked Lauren, however he still communicated with another girl in Queensland who he had begun talking to via the internet when he was back in Forster.

As the old truck pulled up outside Lauren's home, she was waiting for him at the gate. Lauren thought how smart he looked as he jumped out of the truck and waved goodbye to Art. She rushed up to him and threw her arms around him, which sent his big hat flying. As she stooped to pick it up, Chris patted her on the bottom. They walked into the house laughing.

"I missed you, Chris; it's been a whole week. I kept ringing Roma. I was nearly going to ring your aunt. Are you hungry? I got a pizza supreme."

They decided to veg out in front of the TV. Lauren's dad had gone out and wouldn't be back until the next day. Grabbing the pizza, the young couple sat down to watch the latest video, *'Saving Private Ryan.'*

As the movie progressed, he put his arm around her and his hand brushed against her breast. He felt her nipple harden. The next minute they were in each other's arms, the movie forgotten. Lauren just could not keep her hands off him. They tumbled onto the bed, laughing as they urgently shed their clothes. They were soon naked. Quickly he entered her. With a gasp of delight, she pushed against him, lost in the utter bliss of feeling him moving deep within her. They were lost in the excitement and the utter pleasure of each other's bodies.

Later that night as Chris lay there thinking about the future, his thoughts turned to Rachel, the mysterious person he had not met in the flesh. Their friendship consisted of chatting on the net. She lived in far off Queensland, and he suddenly felt like he wanted to check her out.

As the work ended at Bingala, it was time for Chris to move on. He had decided to go to Queensland to spend some time with his pop, his dad's father He thought he might go on to see Rachel, who lived near Hervey Bay, and check out the trawlers for work.

Late in the afternoon Roma and Chris pulled up outside the travel agent where the Brisbane bus was parked. Chris climbed out of the Ute and placed his bag into the luggage compartment. He had on his jeans, red shirt and yes, that big black hat. He was about to board the bus when Lauren came running down the street.

"Chris! Chris! Wait!" She threw her arms around him and sobbed, "Come back, come back soon," kissing him goodbye. He gently broke away and stepped into the bus.

As the shadows lengthened and the warmth of the sun faded, the bus passed the RSL and crossed the Manilla River. Chris found a seat at the back of the bus.

"Can I sit here?" he asked the young lady sitting by the window.

Glancing up at the lean, tanned blond young man, the stranger smiled warmly. "Sure, Curly. I love the hat."

He sat beside the young lady on the bus and began talking to her.

"How ya doin'? The name's Chris," he said.

"Not bad, my name's Tammy, whereabouts are ya heading?" she said with interest.

"I'm looking for a change of scenery. I get off the bus at Brisbane, but from there I guess I'll just take it as it comes."

She smiled and told him how she wished she could just pack up everything and move around like that. They continued talking long into the night and finally both fell asleep somewhere just south of the border.

The bus screeched to a stop at 6 am in Roma Street, Brisbane. Chris didn't have to catch a train for an hour, so he asked Tammy if she'd like to get a coffee. They sat and talked briefly. Chris asked Tammy if he could get her mobile phone number so that if he was ever in Brisbane he could give her a call and they could maybe catch up. They exchanged phone numbers and she said, "Bye Curly."

Chris left on his way to find the right platform to catch his train. He purchased his ticket and scrambled to the station with his stripy reffo bag. He only just caught his train on time, sat down and began to think about work opportunities in Queensland. He had been thinking about going back and working on the sea again. When the train left the Caboolture platform he rang his Grandfather on his mobile asking him to pick him up at Landsborough. The time passed and eventually his stop came and with stripy bag in hand and big black hat donned, he walked off the train to see his grandfather waiting there.

"How ya doing, Pop," he said wearily.

"Not too bad, how have ya been. Ya sound tired, better throw ya stuff in the back an' we'll make a move."

So off they left and returned to his pop's place in the small mountain town of Maleny. His grandfather had told him he could stay with him long enough to get his stuff together and find some work. When they arrived, he threw his possessions in the spare room and decided he'd catch up on some sleep.

The next morning when he woke and walked out into the dining room, his grandfather greeted him. He presented him with muesli and a fruit smoothie he had concocted from nearly every fruit under the sun.

"Bloody hell, what's that?" he asked as if it were half poison.

"Just drink it, you know it's good for you," his grandfather replied as he downed his smoothie concoction.

"Are you going to be heading towards the coast any time soon, Pop? I was thinking I might get back into working on the trawlers," said Chris to his grandfather.

"Chris, you know I don't like you working out at sea, anything can happen, but still I know I can't stop you," he replied. "I'll be heading up near Hervey Bay next week, so I suppose you can have a look around up there."

After much anticipation, the time finally came and they were heading to Hervey Bay. Chris had decided to pack his bags as he was extremely spontaneous to say the least. If he could find the right combination of a good skipper and nice boat, he'd ask if he could move on straightaway, so they could leave port as soon as possible. He'd also thought it would be a good time to meet up with Rachael, his internet friend.

They arrived in Hervey Bay. Chris's grandfather dropped him down at the marina and told him he'd be busy for about three hours and that he'd give Chris a call when he was ready to pick him up if he wanted. Chris agreed and watched his grandfather drive off, turned towards the marina, smiled and rubbed his hands together.

"Home, sweet home," he said to himself. He tried to contact Rachael but her mother said she had left to work in Brisbane.

Chris' passion had always been the sea, either at the beach or working out; it had always made him feel comfortable. He walked down to the jetty and started enquiring about work, explaining that he had experience but that it had been a few months since he'd worked on a trawler. After getting knocked back about four times he was finally given the number by another skipper, who had a mate that needed crew.

So he paced back and forth on the jetty while he called the skipper, eager to start work. He arranged to meet him down at the boat and after a quick inspection of the boat, Chris agreed to work on board. The boat went out to sea for a week at a time. When he returned to port, he would have a lot of money behind him and could do whatever he wanted.

His grandfather rang and told him that he would be down in fifteen minutes to pick him up. Chris explained to his grandfather that he had found work on one of the boats and would be living on it. His grandfather dropped off his bags and told him he'd only be a call away,

"And for Christ's sake, KEEP IN TOUCH!" he said.

A few months went by and Chris was starting to feel unhappy about the way his boss was acting towards him, and he told his boss if he didn't change how he treated him he'd be looking for another crew. The boss was unhappy with Chris' remarks and told him to get his stuff off the boat and find somewhere else to work. So he gathered up his belongings and walked off the boat

'Time for a change of scenery,' he thought to himself. He still had a bit of money left over from the past two trips and decided to travel down to Mooloolaba on the Sunshine Coast. Chris was a unique character; he was unable to be persuaded to pay for anything unless it involved alcohol or a good night. So with his bags over his shoulder he made his way out to the highway and began hitchhiking south.

It wasn't long before a car pulled over to the side and the driver asked, "Hey, where ya off to?"

"Trying to make my way down to Mooloolaba. You heading anywhere near there?" replied Chris.

"Yeah, jump in," the driver said. A few hours passed and then Chris was in Mooloolaba. He shook the guy's hand and thanked him for the lift and they parted ways. It was getting dark and he had nowhere to stay. He sat down by the beach and tried to think about where he was going, when all of a sudden the phone rang. He looked down at the caller ID. He couldn't believe his luck,; it was Tammy, the girl on the bus up from New South Wales.

"Hey, how ya doin'?" Chris answered.

"Not too bad, what have ya been up to?" she asked.

Chris explained his story as to what he'd been up to working out at sea and how he and his former boss hadn't seen eye to eye.

"Really, what a coincidence. I've just moved up to Kawana Waters, the next town down from Mooloolaba," Tammy said with excitement in her voice. She explained how she didn't know anyone in her new town and asked if Chris would like to catch up sometime.

"Sure, there's only one problem, I'm going to get a job on either a tuna boat or a prawn trawler, so I'll be out at sea for a while, but if ya'd like to catch up tonight, I'd love to come round and we can have a few drinks or something," Chris said.

Chris considered himself quite good with words and thought if asked in the right way nothing was out of reach.

Tammy was concerned about bringing back to her place someone she had only known for such a short time.

"Don't worry," he said. "I'll be a perfect gentleman. I'll have most of my stuff with me, 'cause I only just arrived in Mooloolaba about thirty minutes ago."

"OK, I guess I can trust you, just be good or you're out."

"No worries, where do you want to meet up?" replied Chris.

"There's a tavern near my place called Kawana Waters Hotel. If you can make your way there, I'll be waiting for you," she told him.

"Too easy, I'll be there soon, talk to ya then," Chris responded, as he ended the call and picked up his bags.

He walked to the nearest bus stop and waited for the next bus. Soon enough a bus arrived with Kawana Waters on the front. He paid the driver and sat down the back. He watched as his new town rolled past him in a slideshow fashion. He couldn't believe his luck with Tammy calling; it was like something straight out of the movies. He rested his head on the back of the seat and drifted off into a sea of thoughts about what he was going to do. He'd heard that Mooloolaba nightlife was pretty good, so that was swimming around in his thoughts. He was so deep in thought that he'd lost track of time when out of the corner of his eye, he spotted a pub. As he turned his head, he read the sign on the top of the building, which read Kawana Waters Hotel.

He shot up out of his seat and pushed the button to signal the bus driver to stop. The bus stopped about two hundred metres down the road but he didn't mind. It would give him a chance to walk off a bit of the edginess he'd worked up, just thinking about meeting Tammy again.

He arrived at the foyer of the hotel and asked if he could just leave his bags behind the counter, as he was meeting someone. The lady behind the counter smiled and told him it would be fine and so he walked into the pub and ordered a drink and began looking for Tammy.

It was a Wednesday night so there weren't too many people there. He walked around the whole place and couldn't find her anywhere, so he sat down and waited at the bar. Half an hour had gone by and he was beginning to give up hope, when he felt a tap on the shoulder. He turned round to see Tammy standing there.

"Hi what's doin'? I was beginning to think you weren't going to show," Chris said.

"Yeah." She paused. "I wasn't going to but I thought I'd take a risk for once, you know?"

"Yep," Chris replied, "I do that every day, well at least try to."

Chris explained that he would get a room at the hotel and they'd have a few drinks there. He could see she felt much better about that and watched her gradually loosen up and relax. They talked for a few hours and kept drinking. Finally Chris said he was going to go to bed soon because he needed to get up early and look for work. She didn't want him to leave and asked if maybe they could get a few takeaways and head back to his room for a little while. They made their way up to his room and bought a bottle of Bundaberg Rum on the way from the bottle shop outside. They walked up the stairs together and he opened the door. He walked into the room and looked around. There was a small bar fridge, a queen size bed, a bedside table and a TV.

He turned to Tammy and said, "I guess ya get what ya pay for."

He sat his bags in the corner of the room, pulled the table from round the side to the foot of the bed and pulled two glasses out of his pocket that he'd smuggled from the pub downstairs.

She looked at him with a grin. "I didn't even notice you get those."

He winked and told her that he had a feeling he might need them. He poured up two drinks and sat back on the bed; it was almost midnight. They kept talking for a little while until there was a short silence. Chris, oblivious to Tammy's excellent use of self control, decided to turn on the TV. He looked up at the screen and put the remote down on the bed. He watched the screen for two seconds, before Tammy grabbed the remote and turned the TV off.

"Hey!" Chris said in an agitated voice, as he turned to Tammy. She threw the remote, jumped on Chris and began kissing him. They climbed further up onto the bed and Tammy took her shirt off and kneeled above Chris. She took his shirt off and began kissing his chest, while he was grabbing at her breasts. They both stripped down naked and climbed under the sheets as he thought to himself, '*So much for an early night.*'

The next morning he walked down to the marina at Kawana Waters and started asking about work. There were a lot of yachts down there so maybe he might get some slip work, but really he preferred to be out on the sea. He met a man named Ian Nye, who didn't skipper a boat but owned two. Chris gave him his mobile number and told him if he needed any work, to call him.

Nearly a week had gone by and Chris hadn't heard anything. He was beginning to wonder whether coming to Mooloolaba had been the right choice. He decided to be persistent and give Ian a call, as he knew that if he owned two boats, it was only a matter of time before he needed crew. Ian told him that one of the deckhands was leaving in a few weeks' time and told him if he wanted the job he had to go down in the morning and start working on the boat before he did a trip. Chris agreed and was down there the next morning.

The late Ross F. Irwin, "Footy" Captain of the "Lauren G"

Finally, the deckhand left and Chris moved his stuff from the hotel to his new boat, the *Galaxy*. Chris was loaded up with three weeks' supply of tobacco, some new CDs and a new 'Crusty Demons' tee-shirt that cost him $90.

Over the next three months, he did three trips on the *Galaxy*. Ian called him into the office and asked him if he would serve on their sister ship the *Lauren-G*.

Chris said, "Too easy."

The crew of the *Lauren-G* was skippered by a Kiwi called Footy, named after the cartoon 'Footrot Flats' along with the other deckie, Sol. The trio got on well together and made a great team, bringing in lots of prawns.

Early in April '06, a swell developed to the north; the edge of Cyclone Larry. They had been out to sea for twenty days and were returning the next morning with a full load in the brine tanks. But the boys could not let the last night pass without dropping the nets for one final pass on the grounds that had served them so well for the past few nights.

The boys were anxiously watching the storm clouds rolling across the northern skies and the swell gradually increase. At that stage Footy was getting restless and wanted to up nets and return to port as he had just received warnings of high seas and strong wind issued by the weather bureau. The boys started to hoist the nets as the rain pelted down and the wind was reaching thirty knots.

The Lauren G

Everything was going the way it usually did, until they tried to bring the nets on board when they noticed that the centre net was being weighed down. Finally, Sol and Chris brought the net up to the deck to be confronted by a bomb. At least it had been discharged. As they tried to secure it to the deck to dispose of later, Chris slipped and sprained his ankle. Sol and Footy got Chris to the top deck bunk, bandaged his ankle and idled back to port.

Ian gave Chris the next few weeks off to rest before returning to work. Chris was watching the TV on Saturday night when a news flash showed the prawn trawler. The *Lauren G* had sunk while trawling off the Sunshine Coast. The skipper was unaccounted for but the two deckhands were rescued. The news flash reported that the nets had caught something on the bottom and within seconds, the boat had flipped throwing the two lads into the water. The skipper had been in the wheelhouse calling one of the owners to permit him to cut the net.

The search had continued all that day but they had found no trace of the skipper. Chris sat in shock, thinking that except for his accident he would have been on the *Lauren-G*. It was time he moved on; he would look for work out west. Something his mate Sol used to say was ringing in his ears: "Time and tide waits for no man." He saw this as an omen, and decided to give the fishing game up. Chris, being the restless type, couldn't sit still, so that night he decided to go out to his local waterhole, drown his sorrows and drink one for Footy. He had called Sol to meet him at the pub for a few drinks and talk over what had happened.

"Sol, how are you?" Chris said.

Shaking and sweating, Sol finally sat down as Chris handed him a schooner. "I think I'll give the sea away, Chris. That was scary; not only did I have to save myself but young Nat. He was terrified but you can't blame him as it was his first trip."

"Can you tell me what happened?" said Chris as Sol downed his second beer.

"Well, we set out to sea that afternoon, the sea was calm and it was easy going. We headed out to our regular ground and arrived just before sundown. We threw the nets over the side and lowered them to the ocean floor, just like any other trip we had worked on, and everything seemed to be going OK. We went into the cabin for a quick bite to eat, then the new deckhand, Nat, and I went and tried to get a bit of sleep before a hard night's work. A few hours later, we were both awake and getting ready to get the nets up from the bottom, when the boat shifted course and swung round to one side. We knew what had happened. We had hooked up on something big on the ocean floor. I shouted out to Nat and we both ran out the back to see what we could do. Footy had already slowed the revs down and was on the phone to Ian to get permission to cut the nets, but it seemed to all be too late. The boat shifted down onto one side and waves began crashing over the side."

Chris got Sol another beer, and Sol finally got his breath and continued.

"Chris, it happened in a flash. Before we could reach the hand-held GPS, the boat was over. It completely capsized and we were both thrown into the water in the blink of an eye. I looked around, couldn't see young Nat. We were both trapped underneath the boat in pitch darkness. Young Nat told me later that he panicked and he thought that was the end. He had only worked on the boat for less than a day, but he still knew the layout of the deck and finally he made it out of the tangle and miraculously swam out from underneath the canopy, somehow avoiding all the wires and debris. He had already been underwater for over a minute and was running out of breath. He stayed motionless and tried to gain his bearings by feeling which way he was floating and after a second or two, he knew which way was up, and so swam up towards the surface. He said the last five seconds of swimming felt like an eternity, but eventually he surfaced and heard me calling out. "Nat...Footy...' So he yelled, "Sol, I'm over here! Where are you? I can't see anything." So I called back, "Swim towards my voice, the life raft just surfaced over here," trying to sound as confident as I could. Nat swam towards my voice until finally we were both on the life raft.

"Where's Footy?" we asked in unison. We'd both just realised the skipper hadn't surfaced, so we both started screaming out, "Footy!" But our worst fears were realised. As each second went by, it was clear that he wasn't coming up. We both sat there in silence contemplating what had just happened. Seconds turned to minutes and gradually to hours. Finally young Nat turned to me and asked what I thought of the situation and whether or not I thought this might be the end.

"You can't think like that," was my response. "You gotta stay positive. We'll be all right, they'll come looking for us." Sure enough, after a few hours had passed, we were finally spotted by the *Galaxy, Lauren-G*'s sister boat. We were ecstatic, but we also still had mixed emotions about the last ten hours."

"Are we bloody glad to see you!" the skipper of the boat said. "The whole fleet is out here looking for you..." All of a sudden he stopped, his face dropped and he turned white as he realized that Footy was nowhere to be seen.

"Let us just get you two on board and warm," he said as he extended an arm out toward the life raft. They both climbed onto the vessel, sat down and had a cup of coffee. Neither of them wanted to talk about it yet. They were all still coming to grips with the fact that they had lost their skipper. One of the other deckhands came up from below to the forecastle with a couple of blankets. They both wrapped themselves up and drank their coffees. Young Nat tried to lie down and sleep, but the shock still had his brain racing; he just lay there, staring into space. He lay there until they were back in port. Ian, the owner of the boat, was standing there ready to meet them, with the police and ambulance.

The paramedics did a quick physical to make sure they were all right, while one of the police officers tried to get details. However, before they could say anything the paramedics had them both in the back of the ambulance and rushed them off to the hospital. They just wanted to keep them under twenty-four-hour observation. The police officer met Sol and Nat at the hospital and asked them a few questions, but they both had the same answer because it had all happened too quickly. Before they knew it, the boat had flipped and it was as simple as that. The officer wrote down notes and got what he could before leaving. Sol decided to leave and go home; he had had enough excitement for one week.

Chris sat there that night and thought about the boat *Lauren-G*. He began to think back about the girl in Barraba he'd met called Lauren. It was getting late and he'd decided it was time to get away from the coast and head back to the bush. He was about to call his grandfather for a lift back to Maleny when he noticed a girl in country style attire across the room glancing at him every once in a while. He wasn't religious, but he couldn't help but see the signs of something higher pulling it all together in front of him. He paused for a second while he thought back to the Lauren in Barraba, and then the boat he was almost on that sank, *Lauren- G*, and now this country girl casually throwing glances in his direction. It was a full circle that all seemed linked.

So he limped over to start a conversation.

"So, do you normally wear country clothes, or do you just do it to look good?" he said confidently.

"I come from the country, so yeah I guess I wear it normally," the country girl replied.

"Country eh, well let me show you the beach," he said. "I'm Chris, do you mind if I sit down for a while and join you?"

"Sure, my name's Madeline but call me Maddy" she told him.

He sat down as they continued talking. They talked about the sea for a while and slowly the conversation turned towards the country. Chris explained that he was thinking about heading back to the land as he had done a bit of work in New South Wales before. Maddy then began to tell Chris how her father owned a property out in Cunnamulla, in the south-west of Queensland. Chris thought this was all too freaky as Maddy told him that if he needed work and was interested, she could probably get him a job. So he told her to see what she could do. They continued drinking and talking long into the night.

Chris kept in contact with Maddy over the next week or two, and slowly the process was going through when Maddy contacted him one afternoon and said... "It's time to move on."

Christopher had been living the high life in Kawana Waters. He and Sol along with young Nat had been on a few binges. Chris had bunked down at Sol's place in Nambour. One morning doing some shopping they ran into a girl his Pop had introduced at the florist, her name was Lauren. This had to be a coincidence so she agreed to meet him in her lunch time at MacDonald's. Over a Big Mac, he filled her in with what has been happening with his life She did not believe him how her name kept popping into the story line he was pushing .

"What's with the Roosters football jumper, you a fan?" said Chris.

"You could say that actually I am in love with Luke Ricketson, he's a Roosters star."

"I'm a Manly supporter," replied Chris. "So is my dad and Po. There are those who love Manly and those that hate Manly but that's life."

"What are you going to do with your life now, Chris?" asked Lauren.

"Well I met a girl after the accident who's family live on a sheep property out in western QLD. I'm off to Barraba to see my Nana and hope to venture out to this sheep station and hopefully pick up some work "

"Look there is a game on television to night, Manly are going to lose to the Roosters do you want to come around to watch?" said Lauren.

Chris and Sol agreed and purchased a pizza and a slab of Bacardi and coke. Lauren and her girlfriend lived in a flat at Maroouchydore. The boys turned up right on seven thirty.

Lauren's girlfriend, Rachel said to Chris, "God Curly, where did you get that hat?"

It was a great game. Manly won.

Chris and Sol did the pubs in Nambour then met up again with Lauren and her girlfriend. It looked like there were sparks but boys will be boys and they wanted to be moving on. Lauren was upset that Chris was leaving but he was young and had to cross a few stony creeks as his Pop would say.

Chris hitchhiked to Landsborough and rang his Pop to come and pick him up.

"You're a bugger Chris," said Pop. "We never hear from you, we were shocked to see the prawn trawler go down and we had to ring the Kawana police station to see if you were alive."

"I love you Pop" said Chris.

They continued out to Meadow Road.

"Gee the garden looks great Pop," said Chris.

"Ah well, I work on it, still selling leaves to the florists," replied his grandfather. "Put you reffo bags in the green room and come out and have some lunch."

Chris had three text messages one from Lauren in Nambour telling him to come back soon and a surprise one from Lauren in Barraba and one from Maddy in Western Queensland. He answered all three.

"Gee Chris, you get some messages all from birds I suppose," his grandfather said when Chris told him about the messages.

Chris decided to hitchhike to Barraba. His pop dropped him off on the Kilcoy road. He had no sooner turned around to head back to Maleny when Chris had got a lift.

"How far are you going, Curly?" said the young woman at the wheel.

"Well, I'm off to northern NSW, how far you going?"

"Crow's Nest" she replied.

"God where is that?" asked Chris.

"On the Toowoomba road," she replied. "I'll drop you off at the turn off."

They stopped at Esk for a hamburger and coke and then they climbed into the mountains.

"Look my name is Karen," the girl said eventually.

"G'day, I'm Chris."

"What do you do?" she asked.

"Oh, a bit of this and a bit of that. I just worked on a prawn trawler at Kawana."

"Gee, one went down at Easter, I saw it on the telly," she said.

"Yeah, the Lauren G. I worked on that trawler for a few months but I wasn't on it when it went down"

She remained silent for a while but giving him side glances then she said. "What are you going to do now?"

Chris just looked for a while deep in thought and said, "Don't really know. I've got plans to go out west and work on a sheep station. I met this chick, her father has a spread out near Cunnamulla. But I need a bike license you wouldn't know the trouble I had trying to get a license back a few months ago they kept shifting the goal posts."

Karen pulled up at the junction and explained the route he had to take.

"You turn left and go through Toowoomba," she said. "That'll take you down into NSW."

Chris didn't have long to wait. He no sooner had walked fifty metres when a black Toyota sports car came to a sudden stop.

"Where are you going to mate?" asked the young man driving.

"I'm off to Barraba, that's in NSW by the way. I'm Chris."

The man grinned. "Jump in, mate! Bryans the name I'm heading down to Tamworth to the music festival."

Chris climbed in and put his reffo bag on the back seat.

The music on the car stereo was loud with *'The Pub with no Beer'* and Brian was merrily singing along. Chris thought to himself, *I can't stand Slim Dusty.* The car sped through the city of Toowoomba and was soon eating up the kilometres.

They pulled into McDonalds at Stanthorpe for a quick bite. It was 2pm as they climbed back into the car and the weather was a typical hot summer's day.

"It can get bloody cold here in the middle of winter, even get snow," said Bryan.

The slick car crossed the border into NSW.

Chris said, "Does the train still use this line?"

Bryan who said earlier that he had worked for the Queensland railways said, "No must be about fifteen years. Bloody shame, they spent a fortune getting the railway station at Wallangarra back to its best as a federation grant in 1988, but it's now a white elephant. The Queensland railways do use it to pick up fruit but they'll close it down, you wait and see."

Bryan was on his favourite subject. He said he loved trains, he'd worked on the Gympie to Imbil line picking up Pineapples, back in the 70's.

"I'll put Kenny Rodgers on, I just love Kenny," he said. He went on to explain that he was retired now and loved country music.

As they approached Tenterfield, Chris said, "Radar up ahead."

The Great Western Highway was an uninteresting road to travel on and it was easy to lose concentration and bingo! Next thing you look at the speedo and you're cruising at 140 kilometres an hour. Bryan slowed down as he was running out of penalty points, he said, he'd already lost eight. Another fine and he would lose his license.

"You know Chris, I had an old 64EH Holden," he said. "Best car I ever owned but I finally bit the bullet when I retired and brought this sleek machine. Pick up a lot of chicks! I'm meeting up with a friend from Sydney, she is coming up by bus."

By this time Chris was getting a little bored with Bryan's chatter and he said, "Let me out at Glen Innes, I'll get a lift down the back way through Bingara"

He thanked Bryan as he got out a little later and crossed the Highway and before long he had a lift.

"Where do you want to go, lad?" said the driver, an elderly man in casual clothes.

"Oh, drop me off at the Bundarra corner, would be great, thank you," said Chris.

"I am going to Gravesend. I own the pub there. Are you looking for work? I can get you a job chipping cotton if you're interested."

"It'll be right thank you," replied Chris. "My nana lives at Barraba then I'm off to Cunnamulla, got a job out there on a sheep station."

The drive wasn't long and he reached the corner of the Bundarra road and with his reffo bag over his shoulder, he started to walk. He had gone about a mile down the road and it was now late in the afternoon and he was starting to think he would never get a lift when all of a sudden, a Suzuki jeep pulled up.

"Throw your stuff in the back and climb in," said the youthful-looking man at the wheel. "How far is you going?"

Chris was not quite certain if he should get in but it was getting late and the driver didn't look all bad. After introducing themselves, Stan the driver went on to tell Chris he was meeting a mate in Bundarra and he had to pick up some gear and take it onto Tamworth.

Just then, Stan's mobile phone started to ring and he pulled over to answer.

"Yeah, you said to meet you in town by the old bank. Now what? Okay, we'll be there in about fifteen minutes."

Stan put the mobile back in his pocket and pulled out into the road.

"What was that all about?" said Chris.

"No need for you to worry about it," replied Stan.

They drove through the deserted town. It was full of old closed shops, and were quickly driving down the road to Barraba. The road surface went from bitumen to gravel and it had been a long time since it had any road work done. Chris was starting to look nervous.

"What was that all about, Stan?" he asked.

Stan was busy driving and dodging kangaroos. By this time it was getting dark and he had the lights on. Stan said he was meeting his partner in crime. He was picking up a load of grass had a street value of $50,000 that would eventually make its way to Sydney.

Chris started to sweat. He was not aware of what was about to happen. As the car negotiated its way through the twisted rutted road, it was an eerie scene, as the car finally pulled up off the road near Ship Rock. Stan stepped out of the car and he told Chris to wait where he was. As far as Chris was concerned, he was not going anywhere. He closed his eyes and was drifting off to sleep when all of a sudden there was gun fire and shouting.

Stan had left the car and walked the short distance into the bush and around the rock where he met up with his partners in crime. He only knew them as Derrick and Barry Godbold.

"Well, Well I thought you were still inside," he said to the other two.

His friends had done time chipping cabbages in Grafton

"Have you got the grass?" Stan asked.

"Yeah, but did you bring the money, the $70,000?" said Barry Godbold.

"Hang on, it was fifty grand," said Stan.

"Well, the price just went up," replied Barry.

"Look, I don't carry that sort of loose change around, you'll have to wait," said Stan. He had a revolver in his belt and as quick as a flash, he drew the gun and fired and got Barry in the leg.

"You bastard there was no need to do that!" Derrick drew his gun and fired and Stan fell to the ground holding his stomach.

As the shots rang out Chris sat with a jolt. He opened the door and was about to step out but thought better of it. But he could hear the conversation between Stan and two fellows, then another gun shot. By this time Chris was going to leave the car and escape off into the bush as he opened the car door.

A voice called out. "Well who are you?"

Chris was lost for words and finally said, "What have you done to Stan?" He was unaware not only had he become involved in a major drug smuggling racket but also a people smuggling racket. Chris was marched off to the other vehicle a small van. The door opened and he was pushed in. When his eyes became accustom to the dark there were four males hunched up and although they did not speak he could tell they were terrified.

There was much carrying on outside. They had buried Stan in a shallow grave behind the ship rock. Barry started to complain about his leg and he would need attention soon.

"Look, shut your wingeing, Barry," said his brother. "I'll have a look at it when we unload our passengers."

Finally the van moved off. Chris was unable to move about as it was a rough track but then he realized he had his mobile phone in his pocket. In the dark he opened it up and tried to text a message off.

"Shit!" he said. There was no signal. He was thinking about when he was up here back in 2000, he had come up to Bingala with his uncle Steve. It was about sixty kilometres to Barraba and the road went past the old Woods Reef asbestos mine. It was anyone's guess what was going on. Little did he know that these poor chaps, all illegal boat people were heading for Moree to work chipping cotton.

Chris tried twice to send a text message and finally he was successful and left a message on Lauren's phone. It said, "Help, I've been kidnapped by a gang of crooks. I am travelling in a van towards Barraba from Bundarra, they have shot one already. Tell the police."

Lauren was lying on her bed watching the final of Master Chef, a TV reality show that was a winner with viewers. Her mobile started to flash. It was the latest model that her father had given her for her birthday. She said that she would look at the text in the next add break. Finally she read it and nearly fell of the bed. *Is this for real or some kind of joke?* She thought. She pondered over what to do and finally at the next add break she sent off a text to Chris and said to repeat as she thought it was some king of joke. It was some time before Chris had a chance to reply. Finally he sent off a quick reply that it was for real and please get help.

By this time the van was back on the bitumen and heading for the Barraba turn off. Barry was holding the map and told Derrick to turn right, they had to go to Bingara then turn left.

Lauren sent her friend Sam a text that she had just got a text from that young spunk that was here a few months ago. She told her that she had a strange message from him that he was being held up in a van and he needed help.

Sam was going into town that morning and said to Lauren she would call in. Lauren had received another text from Chris. By this time she had started to get concerned and thought he just might be in trouble. Her father was friendly with the local Sergeant in Barraba and she decided to give him a ring. Sergeant Brown was a good friend of Lauren's father, Norm Suffolk.

"Steady down lass, what's this all about?" he said when he picked up the phone. After she had tried to explain, the sergeant dropped everything and drove around to Lauren's place. She had been trying to contact Chris without success. When the sergeant arrived, Chris had sent another text that read that he just heard the driver say, "Turn left at the next crossing, this will take us to Narrabri."

Sergeant Brown didn't know what to believe, He had been involved with drug busts around this area for close on fifteen years but this was a whole new ball game. So he did what he thought was best, he rang the police at Narrabri and they thought he had been drinking. But they sent out a patrol car on the Bingara road just in case. Unfortunately, they didn't know what kind of truck or van they were looking for. Corporal Dickson and a new recruit a young female constable who had only been on the job a couple of days drove slowly along the road waiting for any vehicle to appear.

Sergeant Brown and his side kick set out from Barraba with sirens blazing. Brown said to his assistant, "You know if this is a false alarm we are going to look bloody stupid."

Back in the van, Barry's leg looked serious and he started to winge. Derrick took one look at it and mumbled, "God I don't know, we are going to have to do something with that leg." He knew a short cut to Moore, couldn't remember the town but it was not that far past the church. He knew he had to turn right, then he saw it. But he also saw the police patrol car.

"Bloody hell Barry, the Fuzz!" he said. "We'll just have to bluff our way through this."

He made the turn off and he was straight onto the dirt. The cops didn't turn off but went straight on. The car Stan was driving was way off the main road and it would have been hidden.

Derrick started to relax. Only a few more mile and they could discharge the illegals.

"This isn't where we are supposed to dropped them off, we'll never get paid," he complained.

"Oh shut Derrick," replied Barry. "We're in deep shit, let's just cut our losses and make a run for it."

He pulled up on a deserted stretch of road.

"Guess we should dump our passengers," he said. He got out of the van, went round to the back and opened the back door. "Ok my friends this is where you get off," he said, pointing at Chris. All the men scrambled out after Chris and stood there, not knowing where they were or what to do.

Chris still had his reffo bag. It was great to be out of the van. He could not believe his luck, he still had his mobile. *Bloody idiots* he thought, *they should had got it off him*. When the van had moved off and was out of sight, he called Lauren.

"Hullo Chris, where in the devil are you?" said Lauren.

"Hullo to you too, I'm fine, just been hijacked."

Lauren handed the phone over to the police constable.

"Constable Woodford here, what's going on?"

Chris told the Constable what he knew about what was going on and although he did not know exactly where he was, he described the journey from the turn off and Bingara. The police radioed Moree and indicated what he thought was the road they had taken. He also radioed the Barraba car that was now on the Narrabri road.

Chris suddenly realized that his mobile had GPS. He quickly dialled back the position to the police. The five illegals none of them could speak English were chatting away in a foreign language and they seemed to have decided to stick with their Australian partner. Chris started to walk back along the road to shorten the journey with his five new friends all chatting away.

God he was hungry, a big Mac would go down well he thought.

He heard the siren before he saw the car. When the patrol car stopped, to his surprise Lauren was sitting in the back. She opened the door and rushed into his arms.

"God Chris, are you all right? I've missed you, I never thought I would see you again!"

This all came out in one sentence. Then Constable Woodford gave Chris a drink and as they were driving back to Barraba, Chris gave the constable all the information he could remember.

A few words echoed on the patrol car radio that indicated that the Moree police had apprehended the van as it drove into the outer suburbs of Moree and that as far as Barry was concerned, he was glad it was all over and all he wanted to do was get that bullet out of his leg. Constable Woodford rang Narrabri station asking for a back up van to transfer the five refugees back to Villawood.

That afternoon, Chris along with constable Woodford drove back along the Bundarra road.

"Around the next bend officer. Look there's that rock. God, it just looks like a ship."

Chris was out of the patrol car and there were the car tracks. It did not take long to get to Stan's car.

"Don't touch anything," said Woodford, just behind him. "The forensics from Newcastle will be on the way to check it out."

It did not take long to find the shallow grave, but to Chris' shock, it was empty. The body was no longer there, it looked like Stan had somehow recovered enough to make a getaway.

While Stan's partners in crime had thought Stan was dead, they had driven off. But Stan in a dazed state rose from the dead and staggered off into the bush, his head hurting badly and he was hungry. He did not have far to go when he came across a dirt road. In the distance he could see a farm house and cattle. He limped on and opened the gate to be welcomed by a mean looking dog.

"Down boy," he called out, terrified the dog would attack him. Then from around the corner came a lady.

"Down Brutus" she said. "Can I help you? You look like you have been in an accident." The young lady helped Stan and guided him to the veranda. "Do you want to talk about it? My name is Cathy Moran. My god, you're bleeding!"

Stan collapsed on the front step Cathy called out to her young brother to give a hand and before long they had him sitting in a chair.

"I think what you need is a strong cup of tea," said Cathy.

"Something stronger would be nice" said Stan.

Cathy went into the house and said to her brother, "Mick, we should call an ambulance."

"A lot of good that will do sis," replied Mick. "You know what they will say, is it urgent, how bad is he hurt, they have to come from Armidale and they will be at least two hours."

"Don't worry," said Cathy. "I'll have to tell them he has been involved in a gun fight, that will get them out here and fast."

With that, she picked up the phone and dialled the emergency number.

Mick put a rug around Stan and gave him a stiff drink of their father's home brew whiskey.

"God, Cathy," said Stan, downing the drink in one gulp. "That would kill a brown dog! what is it?"

But the drink had an effect and Stan got drowsy from the fatigue and shock for twenty minutes. But he woke up sharply as an ambulance drove through the gate, followed by a police car.

In the car on the way back to Barrabba, all Lauren was concerned with was to get her lover boy home to her place and give him a beer and something to eat. So on the way, she got the sergeant to stop off at the takeaway for some hamburgers. As soon as the police car had stopped, the local press was there with cameras.

"Young miss, what you can tell us about the crime scene?

The sergeant was out of the car in a flash.

"Sorry Brian," he said firmly, "no comments. I'll give a full report in the morning at the station".

"Gee Chris," said Lauren, "you'll be a celebrity! You might get onto *'The Morning Show'* on Channel 9!"

"Right now darl, I just need a shower and one of those burgers," replied Chris.

Chris took out the mobile phone and called his Nana at White Hut and tried to explain what had happened.

"No worries Nana, will see you in the morning," he said and ended the call.

Chris spent the next week at White Hut helping Arthur with work around the property. He had a visit from the local police trying to piece together the drug raid and if Chris could give them any more information. Lauren was on the phone everyday hounding Chris to come in to see her. Finally after a week Arthur drove him into town. He had been on the phone to Maddy in Cunnamulla to see if the work was still on. He had finally had his motorbike license it was a must for the work out there.

Lauren met him at the front door with a hug as Chris waved Arthur off. She had gone to a lot of trouble making a three course meal. But she was in a hurry to get him into bed. They made passionate love like there was no tomorrow.

"Chris why do you want to go off and leave me? You know I love you to bits," she said after a quiet time as they hugged each other.

"I just have to go," replied Chris. "You know me, always on the move. Now, what about that dinner?"

And Lauren had to be content with that.

Chris had phoned Cunnamulla before leaving White Hut and he was to start as soon as he got there. Lauren was going to borrow her father's Ute and drive him to Moore where he would catch a bus to Goondiwindi then finally a bus would take him to Cunnamulla.

Chris's Uncle Steve was working on a sheep and cattle property near Terry Hie-Hie. So the young couple set out to drive to Moore and call in and see his uncle on the way.

As the four wheel drive drove into the main street of the town, Chris said, "Where is everybody?"

Lauren chuckled. "Look Curley, this is the bush! What you see is what you get."

They found the off road that Steven worked in and after five kilometres they arrived at the front gate. Chris could see his uncle down in the paddock and called out to him as they drove in. Steven directed them to his place set behind the shearing shed.

"How you going you old bugger?" said Chris.

"Cut out this old!" replied Steven. "I could still give you a licking, you young whippersnapper!"

Chris brought his uncle up to date on the drama of the past week.

"Yeah, we heard all about it," said Steven. "The cops finally caught up with some of the mob not far from here."

Steven went on and asked Chris if he was looking for work.

"I've got something happening at Cunnamulla," replied Chris. "My good friend Lauren is driving me to Moore then I'll probably pick up a bus. Gee uncle, have you got a VB?"

"No, sorry Chris, but how about a cupper and you better meet the missus, Debbie."

They did not get away till after five o'clock. Steven suggested they stay at the hot pool in Moore.

They rented a unit and spent the next few days frolicking around in the warm water. Lauren didn't want to leave.

"Chris don't go, stay with me and we will find a farm that you can work on," she said sadly.

"Sounds cool," said Chris. "But I have given my word and Maddy said her father will want me for at least six months."

"Gee Chris I thought you loved me," whispered Lauren and with that she started to cry and turned away so Chris could not see her disappointment.

"Gee love, don't cry I promise I'll return," said Chris.

On their last night together they made passionate love and fell asleep tightly wrapped in each other's arms.

The next day, there was silence as Lauren drove the Tarago down to the bus station. Lauren felt that things had happened last night and that she hadn't seen the last of Curley. She waved the bus off as it went down the main street of Moore.

The bus passed the town of Boggabri, the last town in NSW before crossing the Macintyre River into Queensland. There were aboriginal kids diving off the bridge into swollen water and Chris looked enviously at them, he thought it looked fun.

When the bus reached the station, he found that he would have a four hour wait for the bus that was travelling west. The bus station was down near the river and as he left the bus he was propositioned by some hoodies for a fag and some grass. Chris was having none of that. After his last few days he was staying clear of trouble. But he decided to go over to the pub for a beer as he he was thirsty.

As he crossed the road, he thought of the situation with Lauren. How was he going to get out of this one? Over his short life he had escaped any real commitment with women, his idea was love them and just leave them, it had worked in the past.

It was nearly five pm when the Greyhound bus finally pulled up.

"How far are you going, Curley?" asked the driver.

"There and back," replied Chris. "But Cunnamulla will do for a start."

"Cheeky bugger! Where are you working in Cunna?" said the driver.

Chris really didn't have a clue, all he knew that he was to ring Maddy the moment he arrived in town. He took a seat behind the driver and watched the countryside pass by. He began chatting with the man at the wheel and had a great old conversation with him. He told him about the raid over the last couple of weeks. Jock, the driver told Chris it was in all the papers out here. Chris was a celebrity, it seemed.

The Greyhound bus arrived at the bus station at nine forty five. As Chris got off the bus with his reffo bag over his shoulder, the driver said, "Best of luck, Curley, don't get into any mischief out here. The station owners have big guns and they know how to look after their daughters."

Chris just laughed and gave him a wave. He looked around but there was not a soul there to greet him so he wandered off to the pub. He made a phone call on his mobile to his only contact, Maddy, but no answer. He asked the barman if he knew of a young lady called Maddy, her parents ran a cattle and sheep station somewhere around here.

Straight away, the barman knew what Chris was on about.

"Sonny, you probably mean the Matheson spread," he told Chris. "Yeah, it's about fifty clicks. You got a motor bike have you, 'cos you will need one to work on that spread."

"Don't talk about motor bikes," replied Chris. "The motor rego put me through hell. Six times, I went for the test, they kept changing the rules. I got lucky and got it, no sweat in Barraba. I think the officer took pity on me in the end and just passed me to get rid of me."

"Hi Curley, are you Chris?" asked another barman who had just answered the phone. "Jim Matheson's manager is on the line, says to stay here for the night and someone will be here in the morning and the station will pay."

"Gee thanks," Chris replied.

"When you're ready, bunk down in unit number six," said the barman. "Better go to the kitchen and get something to eat."

Next day, bright and early Chris was out at the front of the pub.

God it was hot! he said to himself. It was thirty degrees already and it was only eight am. A great flock of silver crested galahs took off, screeching their heads off. Then a blue Land Rover pulled up, skidding to a halt. Then a gorgeous blonde girl jumped out.

"Hi! You must be Chris! I'm Janice, Maddy's sister. Look, I've got a few things to do in town, so hop in and I'll give you a quick tour of Cunna."

Somewhat tongue-tied at the beautiful vision, Chris just nodded and climbed into the passenger seat of the Land Rover, trying not to stare too hard at Janice.

The tour of the town didn't take long. Janice had to pick up some farm medicine and they were off. As they drove out onto the main road and into the unrestricted speed zone, she wound the four wheel drive up to nearly the maximum speed it could reach.

"Do you always drive fast out here Janice?" asked Chris, feeling nervous.

"Yeah, but only in the daylight hours because around sunset, it's murder!" she said with a laugh. "Wildlife of all kinds, all over the place!

As the four wheel drive pulled up at the front gate to the property, Chris was surprised.

"Gee, that was quick!" he said.

She laughed. "Don't worry, it's another forty clicks to the homestead," she said as she got out and checked the post box which was a forty-four gallon drum on its side with a lid to keep out nasties. "We get stuff most days," she continued as she got back behind the wheel and set off again. "There's been no rain, it's been a horribly dry summer and bush fires are always a worry," she said as she drove along the unsealed track. She turned and looked at him. "What was your last job, Chris? God, you have a great crop of curly hair!"

"Yeah I know, I get Curley all the time," Chris replied with a grin, finally feeling at ease with this beautiful woman. He went on to tell Janice of his time on the Lauren G and its drama.

"You know, you're lucky," said Janice. "We need some extra help now with the mustering. Our flocks are spread far and wide right out to the Paroo River. Do you know, Chris, you can ride all day from one side of the property to the other side, it's that big."

"How big is big?" asked Chris, intrigued by what she was telling him.

"Over 50,000 acres," she said. "That's small compared to some of the properties further out, but big enough. We're also building a feed lot run. Have you ever done any building, Chris?"

"Not a lot, but I helped my Nana back in Barraba. They have a few acres and she runs horses so we were always fixing stables."

After another twenty minutes, the homestead came into view.

"Mum and Dad are away at present," said Janice. "So there's only my sister Maddy and Geoff here at the moment. I'll take you over to you accommodation. It's a Donga, quiet nice air con and TV reception, nothing but the best and then I'll introduce you to Brad, he's our head stockman and he'll fill you in on you pay and hours."

She drove behind the house and stopped outside a neat-looking cottage. She got out and led Chris inside and he dropped his bag, admiring the comfortable space with a bed and a good-sized television set.

"I'll leave you here to relax and wind down," Janice said and to Chris' regret, walked out again.

Late that afternoon, Brad and his team returned back and Janice came and got him and introduced him to the team. They were having a BBQ that evening. All of a sudden, like a whirlwind, a smart Subaru sports car pulled up with dust flying everywhere. Young Maddy flew out of the machine and raced straight over to Chris, threw her arms around him and hugged him.

"Hi gorgeous!" she said loudly. "Great to see you again!"

Startled, Chris realised she was probably even more beautiful than Janice and decided he was a very lucky man indeed.

The rest of the evening passed in a whirl of new faces, talking to Brad and his team, with Chris trying to get closer to Maddy all the time and not finding it easy with competition from the guys around.

Early next morning as the sun was just breaking the horizon, Chris was woken by Brad knocking on his door.

"Are you awake Chris? Rise and shine, we have work to do!"

Chris dragged himself out of bed, flung on his jeans and tee-shirt and went out to meet the crew and be given a rundown of the work to be carried out. Brad gave the order to one of the team, Spike, to take Chris in the Jeep after lunch and check the south boundary fence and to take supplies for two days.

Before they left, Maddy finally surfaced and took Chris to one side and explained that she was glad to see him but she was off to Brisbane to Uni. She was starting a course in vet science. They all gathered on the veranda of the work shed for lunch. There were five workers on the station.

So just after one pm, Spike and Chris set out in the jeep. Spike started to tell Chris about his life in the city and how he got this job while he was doing time in Odyssey House.

"Yes I know what you are thinking Chris, I was a drug addict."

"Aw gee, I've come pretty close myself," said Chris. "My problem is grog. I'm going to try to stay clear of it."

Spike nodded in understanding.

The work plan was for them to drive around the fence line checking for damage, water troughs and any problems they could see. They were in radio control with Brad at the base. They had gone about half an hour and stopped at a damaged part of the fence and repaired it.

"Pigs," said Spike. "Bloody major problem out here, they cause all sorts of problems. They also bring in disease. You know, we're worried about pigs that have been introduced from New Guinea and bring all sorts of diseases."

There also seemed to be rabbits everywhere.

Chris said, "Whatever happened to the Calicivirus that was supposed to eradicate the problem?"

"They still taste all right," said Spike with a grin. "You can have a right old fun time shooting them."

It was just on dusk when they pulled up and made camp for the night. They'd repaired several more fence patches, cleaned up and refilled water troughs and reset a few fence posts that had sagged over to one side. Chris was buggered but he was not saying anything. They sat around the fire drinking tea and finally the subject got around to girls.

"We sometimes go into Cunna," said Spike. "But except for the pub there's nothing. About six months ago, some girls turned up in a caravan and set up on the edge of town but the Fuzz soon moved them on."

Before he could continue, out of the stillness came a howl.

"Dingos," said Spike. "Don't worry, they won't come near us as long as we keep the fire going."

Eventually, they rigged the small tents they had brought with them and turned in. Chris slept like a log but woke refreshed in the morning. As he climbed out of the tent, in the early morning mist it the distance, something moved. He rubbed his eyes, thinking he was seeing things. It looked like a cat, a bloody big cat and pitch black. He quietly spoke to Spike who had just climbed out of his tent.

"Over there Spike. God, what is it?"

Spike was still rubbing sleep from his eyes. "What are you on about, Chris?"

"Over there," said Chris. "Look at it, it's not a feral cat, it looks like a panther."

Spike grabbed his binoculars and took a better look. He caught a glimpse of something as it went into stand of trees.

"God, I think you're right, Chris. Mind you, there have been sighting over the years about big cats all over the far north Queensland. It all started just after the Second World War. There were American army units bivouacking through here and some of them had some unusual pets for mascots. Remind me to ring base and tell them. Also I'd better ring our neighbours at Glendilla Station. Although there have been sightings over the years, there's never been any attacks on stock that have been identified. You'll always get dog attacks, they can maul a sheep to pieces, but nobody has ever thought it was a big cat attack."

As they wandered over to the trees to see if they could catch a glimpse of the animal. Spike had the rifle ready, but the animal had disappeared.

"Spike, how did you got that name?" asked Chris.

"When I was school, I had a special hair cut and the name stuck," said Spike. "My real name is - wait for it – Murray!"

With friendship established, the boys spent the next two days driving the boundary until they reached the western boundary, the Paroo River. It had been a hot afternoon and they stripped and went for a dip in one of the pools.

Chris spent the next few months working on the station doing everything from mustering, pulling sheep out of the dams and his favourite pastime, getting around on the trail bikes. He also helped on the stock yard enclosure and the feed troughs. They made it into the hotel in Cunna most weekends but by Friday night they were too exhausted to go anywhere so they would crack open a few tinnies and there was always fresh meat to barbeque.

He had been there six months when he received a letter from Lauren. He didn't read it till he had finished work and was in his bunk.

It read,

"Dear Chris, I hope this short letter finds you well and I am sad you have not written to me in all the time you have been there. Is Maddy that good, you little shit? Guess what, I'm pregnant and yes you are the father. I have not been with anyone else since we made love in Moore so congratulations. I don't expect you to do anything like race back on a white charger. You have my phone no so how about giving me a ring or a text

I was once your girlfriend, Lauren."

Chris put the letter in his top draw. *God I was never her boyfriend,* he thought, *but I think it's time to move on. Northern Territories, Queensland, they both sound great.* His brother was in Mackay working on the mines. Great money he was always telling him and in his last text he'd said he could earn a grand a week no trouble and that was working above ground. You could double that if you went underground.

Over the next few weeks, he and Spike regularly patrolled the western border of the property.

"You're very quiet Curley, anything wrong?" asked Spike at one point. "Want to talk about it?"

Chris drove for a bit and pulled up under a giant River Gum that was growing on the banks of the river.

"Aw gee, Spike, what can I say," he muttered. "Looks like I've got a girl into trouble and she seems to think I'm the one. I'm not ready to settle down."

"That's a bugger," said Spike sympathetically. Little more was said on the drive back.

As they made their way back to the homestead, they saw there was a big barbeque being set up. The boss and his lady were just back from overseas. The lads had showers and spruced themselves up and made their way over to the pool and open air dining area.

Chris with his letter from Lauren on his mind got into the grog and was away dancing with both Maddy and Janice. Janice was a great mover and although a bit older than Chris, was making eyes and suggestive movements with her body.

"God, you're beautiful and I reckon you'd be great in bed," said Chris, made a bit silly by the beers he'd drunk.

Janice just looked at him and said, "God, Chris, I'm nearly old enough to be your mother!"

"God I thought you were only in you thirties," he replied.

"Yeah, something like that," she said and broke away.

Somehow, Maddy was in his arms.

"She's too old for you, Chris," she said.

With that, it was Chris's turn to break away and he struggled out to the back and was ill. Next morning, he told Brett that he would be finishing up at the end of the month. Brett said nothing but simply nodded.

That weekend, the lads decided to venture into town for some recreation. The boss allowed them time off every other weekend, so they would take sleeping bags as they would camp out somewhere. Now and again, they would get lucky and spend the night in some sheilah's bed.

Jake was taking his Holden EH station wagon. He only ever took it out on special occasions like on a pub crawl. Chris was all decked out in his black Crusty Demons shirt. Several people had said they reckoned he would wear it to bed if he could, and his black hat. Jake made some remark about the hat.

Chris only laughed and said, "You can't talk, look at yours!"

Jake was proud of his battered Akubra and he kept the car better than he would a woman. On the dash board was a bottle opener, although most of the drinks these days were cans. All Chris could see as the miles slipped by was all the empty cans.

Jake read his mind and said, "Chris I know what you're thinking. Once a year we do a cleanup and give all the cans to the Lions club. They make a few bob and last year we filled up three utes."

The pub crawl passed uneventfully, nobody got lucky and they all slept in their sleeping bags that night before returning home with varying degrees of hangovers.

Chris had purchased a Honda 500cc motor bike and he was going to ride it back to Barraba to catch up with his Nana and have a serious talk with Lauren, hoping that she would see if it was not too late to get an abortion. But more immediately, he and Spike set out for their inspection of the southern and western boundary fence. They were in the works four wheel drive Nissan Patrol. They were just setting up their swags and have a quiet drink when there was a radio message over the two-way radio.

"Come in Spike or Chris drama at the homestead, can't talk too much but we have been invaded by a gang of three hoods and they had tied up the boss and are demanding money. Can you get over to Glendilla and ask Joe to call Cunna police station and get help? Signing off, Maddy."

"God, Chris, "We'd better get our fingers out," said Spike in alarm. As quick as a flash they were packed up and off. It was not far to the neighbour's property, but in the dark they could not travel at any speed. They reached Glendilla's gate but it was still a further two kilometres to the homestead. With horns blazing they covered the last few hundred metres in quick time. With all the noise, Joe came out of the bunk house.

"What's up, fellers? You're are going to wake the dead."

Spike spoke first. "Joe, big trouble at our spread. Call the cops and tell them three masked men are holding up the boss and his missus, guns the lot. Chris got a message over the two way"

It didn't take long for the police in Cunna to get onto the case and Chris and Spike along with Joe made their way back to the homestead. They were about 500 metres from the house when they spotted flames leaping in the air.

Spike said, "Looks like they've set the hay bales on fire or the shearing shed."

It was a well known fact that Lanolin was highly inflammable and when ignited, would go up in flames. They parked away from the scene of the crime and crept up in the shelter of a ten acre patch of Paulownias that the family had planted back in 1980. They were going to be a super fast growing tree that was set to take on the world but it never happened so they were left and the cattle loved them. Now they provided good cover.

The three lads were armed with rifles and weren't afraid to use them. As they crept up through the undergrowth, they were only fifty metres from the back of the sheds and could hear everything. Spike spoke first in a whisper.

"Look, there are three of us. Lets wing them. Shoot them in the legs. I'll take the big guy on the left. Chris, you take the middle one and Joe, you take the big fat guy on the right. try not to miss."

As they lined up their targets, sirens started to sound in the hills. One of the crooks called out, "Cops! Bloody hell we cut the phone lines and disposed of their mobiles. Someone blabbed."

It was all over in a few minutes the cops arrived with guns blazing no one was injured.

A few days later, Maddy and Janice put on a BBQ for the crew to farewell Curley. Over the eight months he had been there, he had quickly gained the nick name. It was just after lunchtime when he rode out of the property on his motorbike. He had about six hours ride to Barraba.

God he said to himself, *I'm going to be a dad.* The last text he had from Lauren said she was due in early October. He stopped at Cunna and phoned his Nana. All Roma could tell him was that Lauren was in Barraba hospital, nothing to worry about, but Doctor Raja thought it was wise as it was her first. He pressed on and was in Cunna just as the sun went down. Macca's was open, the sign said open 24 hours. His thoughts turned to his Pop. The old bugger was always onto him about getting married as Chris was his only grandson and he was now after great grandchildren.

It was getting late and he decided to pull into a recreation stop for cars and caravans. He would pitch his tent and climb into his sleeping bag and be off in the morning. He had just dropped off when he was woken by a hand resting on his shoulder.

"Bloody Hell you frightened the daylights out of me! What do you want?"

"Just a little company, I'm lonely," said a female voice.

"How did you get here, anyway?" demanded Chris.

"I'm Gail, shanks pony, gee, you look snug in that bag. Can I join you?"

Chris rubbed the sleep from his eyes. "Come in. Are you cold? If you are, get in to my sleeping bag."

"Gee thanks!" said the woman. "You know, I don't normally just get into bed with anyone. I got a lift with a couple of creeps and I'm trying to shake them off."

She was shivering and as she snuggled up to get warm, she told Chris she had been out at Windorah as a jillaroo for six months. She'd had enough of the owner's son continually pestering her to get into his bed. Strangely enough, nothing happened that night but a pleasantly warm sleep.

In the morning, Gail went to the toilet block to freshen up. Chris pulled the tent down and packed it away on the bike.

"Well, where do you want to go?" asked Chris. "I can give you a lift to Goondiwindi. I'll branch off there to Moore."

"That's fine," she replied. "I'll make my way down the Brisbane from there. I have an aunt there, then I'm off to Rockhampton."

They exchanged phone numbers and they parted at MacDonald's. Chris rang his Nana in Barraba.

"Hi Nana, how are you? I'm at Moree and will be there sometime this avo."

"Chris you better go straight to the hospital," said Roma. "Lauren was admitted this morning."

"Is she alright?"

"Chris, you should have been a little more caring. Young Lauren has hardly heard from you while you have been in Cunnamulla."

"Well Nana, I intend to make it up to her and do the right thing. My brother Jimmy has got me a job in the mines in Mackay and he has accommodation. Anyway, I'm running out of money. Will see you later, I love you."

Some time later, Chris drove into the parking lot at the hospital and was met by Lauren's father.

"Hi Norm, hope she's okay?" said Chris.

"Yes, she's fine, no thanks to you, you young bugger," said Norm. "Anyway, you'd better get into the maternity ward, she's just starting."

"What Norm, you want me to go into the ward and watch the birth?"

"Yes Chris, watch the birth of your child."

Chris was ushered into the ward and decked out in a green gown and nearly passed out. He didn't have long to wait. He had only just got into the gear when he heard a loud scream and a baby's cry.

The nurse came over and said, "Congratulations! It's a boy."

Chris and Norm went out to the canteen and had a coffee. Lauren was not ready to see any one yet. Norm said, "Well son, what are you going to do now? Run off or show some gumption and look after the girl. She thinks the world of you, you know."

Chris just sat there and thought to himself, *Well life had caught up with me.*

Chris stayed at Lauren's place for nearly a month and then they decided he would go north and get set up in the job his brother had lined up for him in a mine at Mackay and send for Lauren and Josh later.

As he set out on his bike, Lauren was all in tears. Her last words were, "Drive safely and don't drink too much and ring me as you go along. Please keep in touch."